Rani Padmavati

Rani Padmavati

The Burning Queen

Anuja Chandramouli

 juggernaut

JUGGERNAUT BOOKS
KS House, 118 Shahpur Jat, New Delhi 110049, India

First published by Juggernaut Books 2017

10 9 8 7 6 5 4 3 2 1

ISBN 9789386228529

Typeset in Adobe Caslon Pro by R. Ajith Kumar, New Delhi

Printed at Thomson Press India Ltd

*For Veda and Varna – my brave,
bright and beautiful boos*

Contents

Contents

Prologue: Murder Most Foul

The shah's flotilla wound its way upriver at a gentle pace towards Kara. It was accompanied by a small cavalry contingent led by Ahmad Chap, who, before the journey, had argued for a bigger force.

'The safety of our sovereign is paramount,' he had said, 'because there are traitors everywhere.'

'You sound like an old nursemaid,' Jalaluddin Khalji, the unlikely ruler who had spearheaded the bloody campaign against the Slave dynasty and destroyed Balban's descendants, had remarked, smiling affably. 'You would have me believe my own shadow is a threat to me! So much so that you'll have me surrounded by bodyguards even when I am emptying my bowels or taking my pleasure with a woman!'

Even though he was nearly seventy, the shah's features

remained pleasing. He was of medium height and nearly as trim as he had been at the peak of his illustrious military career. There was a fragile air about him, a certain placidity which, when combined with his slight limp and the marked asymmetry of his physique due to one battle injury too many, gave people an impression of weakness.

Chap had remained stone-faced amid the mindless titters that always accompanied an emperor's jest, even though it was lacking in real humour and he would be damned before falsely admitting that his concern for the king was absurd.

Jalaluddin took note and sighed. He was sick of people who disapproved of every little thing he had done during the six years of his almost perfect and nearly always peaceful reign. Still, he had to say something to the well-meaning but tiresome man who stood before him.

'Alauddin is like my son. He's never given me cause to doubt him,' the shah began, his voice sounding unflatteringly pompous to his own ears. He was a simple soldier at heart and would never ever get used to being a monarch. 'He has been a good husband to my beloved daughter, though Allah forgive me, she becomes more like her mother with every passing day. Still, he is patient and loving, almost to his own detriment. There is no man I know of who is braver or more honourable than Alauddin

Khalji. And despite what his detractors say, he does not have a greedy bone in his body.'

His courtiers shuffled uneasily.

How could someone so wise be so blind and deaf to the obvious? Chap wondered, swallowing his frustration with effort. Even though he would have liked to convince the shah of the growing threat posed to him by Alauddin, it was not his place to argue.

Alauddin Khalji was a dangerous man, who certainly did not love the king's daughter and had long coveted the Delhi throne. Everybody knew it, with one glaring exception of course. Not only had Alauddin dared to attack Devagiri without the monarch's consent, he had ignored the summons to Delhi, and had somehow convinced the shah to visit him at Kara so the monarch could receive the booty amassed from the fallen kingdom. Why couldn't the shah see the perfectly laid trap? Alauddin had no intention of parting with the ill-gotten treasure that otherwise rightly belonged to his king.

'We do not question your judgement, Sire!' Chap tried again. 'But surely it is better to err on the side of caution? All I ask is that you be surrounded by an armed escort at all times and we march towards Kara in full strength as befits the shah of Delhi.'

Jalaluddin frowned. Yes, he was old and infirm but did they all think he was stupid as well? He could practically hear their thoughts and smell their distrust of his nephew. They had spewed similar poison into his ears regarding the pious and hugely popular dervish Sidi Maula and the treasonous happenings at his khanqah. Jalaluddin had issued the holy man's death sentence, decreeing that he be crushed by a mad bull elephant. The unfortunate incident had left a foul taste in his mouth.

And now his courtiers would have him kill his own nephew and son-in-law for imagined treason and make a widow out of his daughter, who had recently reached out to him with the sweetest tidings. It had taken many years but finally she was pregnant. He couldn't wait to see her. And so the grandfather-to-be decided he would go armed with riches and gifts for his beloved daughter, not take along with him a horde of bloodthirsty troops.

'I will hear nothing further on this subject,' he said. 'Mistrust is a breeding ground for fear, treachery and violence. It is why a son will turn against his father, or a brother against his brother. Such a hateful disease shall not taint my golden reign. I hold my nephew in the highest regard and he will never repay my faith with betrayal!'

That had been that.

The royal barge rounded the bend and soon the shah could discern Alauddin mounted on his horse. Under the scorching sun, his dutiful nephew waited on the stone wharf below the grand fortress, ready to receive him. His entire army was assembled in full uniform for the shah's inspection. The soldier in Jalaluddin was pleased to note that they struck a note of real fear in his heart, which was just as it should be.

He was slightly disappointed too. His daughter was not there to receive him, but she could hardly be expected to be present in her delicate condition. The old monarch had seldom been happier or more at peace. Ultimately, all the treasure in the world was worth nothing next to familial bonds and filial affection.

~

Alauddin watched the untidy assortment of boats swarming up the river, heavily laden with fat nobles, their fatter concubines, endless paraphernalia and accoutrements – ranging from servants and livestock to unwieldy cargo including furniture, artwork and treasure chests – that corrupt and incompetent courtiers could not live without.

The sight of the fleet wallowing in the muck like a pregnant sow turned Alauddin's stomach; it was symbolic of the state of the kingdom which was in a shambles, thanks to that old fool who stood beneath the ornate royal canopy, smiling like an imbecile. The same man who was known to feast with traitors, who had rebelled against the throne and allowed robbers and crooks to go free with nothing more than a slap on the wrist and well-meaning words of advice. Fool!

If that was not bad enough, Jalaluddin had granted a royal pardon to their sworn enemies, the Mongols, who had been taken as his prisoners of war. Not only were they pardoned, they had been allowed to convert to Islam and were given rich tracts of land to settle in! He had even given his own daughter's hand in marriage to one Ulugh Khan, who claimed descent from Genghis Khan.

Words failed Alauddin.

Yet, his disdain wasn't evident on his face even to those who stood closest to him. His features were thickset with extraordinarily crooked teeth that ensured he could never be handsome. He was short of stature and hefty, his physique disproportionate with skinny limbs and a swollen belly. But there was something about his eyes. Those who took note remarked they burned with a fiery passion that lit up his face. And right now, his eyes were gleaming with fierce intent.

Alauddin continued to watch impassively as his man, Almas Beg, accompanied by two skiffs, drew closer to the royal barge. They requested an audience with the king, which was granted with alacrity. Beg was conferring animatedly with the shah, and Alauddin watched in disbelief as the old fart ordered his bodyguards aside, lowering himself onto a smaller boat with the eagerness of a child, urging the rowers to hurry towards the shore. Could he really be that stupid? It was possible the old shah was really anxious to get his paws on Alauddin's hard-earned riches from the Devagiri campaign.

The instant Jalaluddin stepped onshore, Alauddin nodded slightly. His men swung into action to execute their orders with the precision and perfection their overlord always demanded.

It was an exhilarating sight.

A single, clean stroke of a sword and his father-in-law's head rolled onto the muddy banks, eyes agog with surprise. In death, the shah looked even more ridiculous than he had in life. His assailant held the head up to show Alauddin, who nodded in approval.

It was almost over but not quite. The deadly music of swords rang out as Alauddin's soldiers made short work of their allotted victims. The former shah's courtiers and attendants were swiftly executed along with their women and children, their clarion cries for clemency cut off by the assailants.

The river ran red with their blood and Alauddin thought the hue looked most pleasing under the golden rays of the sun. His men on the opposite bank had been busy too, cutting down Chap's forces with embarrassing ease only because, like Jalaluddin, they too were weak and foolishly sentimental. It was all over so swiftly it felt like it had barely begun.

Alauddin's troops raised a great cheer in his honour, even as they brandished the head of his predecessor, which was still dripping blood.

'Long live Alauddin Khalji! Our true king!'

'Born to rule the world and lead us to the very pinnacle of glory!'

'Saviour from the tyrant and the Mongol menace!'

There was more of the same fawning nonsense as his fellow conspirators raised the royal canopy over his head, declaring him the new shah of Delhi, their malice hidden behind fake smiles. Despite being aware of their falseness, there was genuine warmth in Alauddin's eyes as he accepted the accolades that had long been denied to a warrior of his stature, all because of the monarch he had just deposed and his bitch of a daughter whom he had been forced to marry. For that alone Jalaluddin had deserved to die.

Alauddin smiled at some of his courtiers – the plotters who had backed Malik Chajju's revolt against the late Jalaluddin not long ago. As a blood relative of Balban, Chajju had felt entitled to the throne and there were those who had foolishly encouraged him. These conspirators had been pardoned by Jalaluddin. More fool him! And thanks to their machinations, the sentimental sop was now dead. Alauddin wasn't going to make the same mistake. He gave his swordsmen the sign and they gathered around the conspirators.

The new shah did not linger to watch the carnage. There was much to be done. As he rode towards the palace, he was surprised at the wave of sadness that assailed him over the loss of his father-in-law. He would be the first to admit that the doddering, drooling dullard had been good to him and had genuinely been a noble soul. But the unfortunate truth was that the world seldom had any use for virtuous men, especially those who were kind to a fault.

Clearly, even the late shah's daughter did not care too much for him. It was dear Malika Jahan, his wife, who had insisted that Alauddin not hand over the booty from Devagiri to her father. It was she who had hatched this plot with the other conspirators, inducing her father to visit them at Kara with false tidings.

The news about her father's death would have reached her by now. And if he knew his wife well, he was sure she wouldn't be too unhappy about it.

~

He wasn't wrong.

'Thanks to my efforts, a rat-faced, miserable excuse for a man has won the throne of Delhi!' Alauddin's wife spat out the words.

Malika Jahan was nearly a head taller than him, with an ample bosom and an even more abundant rear. She was no great beauty but she was an expert in disguising her flaws. Her mostly effective cosmetic aids included worms, snake venom and goat's blood. Even the red dye she used to paint her lips with was extracted from a rare bloom that was toxic to the touch. Thankfully, Alauddin had never felt the urge to kiss her, or touch her for that matter.

'Don't you be giving yourself airs now!' she continued. 'It would do you good to remember who you have to thank for your ill-deserved good fortune. Don't think I will hesitate to—'

The woman could seldom be stopped mid-tirade but when he struck her across the face, his heavy rings slashing her fleshy cheeks, she shut up at once. She looked every bit as comically surprised as her father had. The magnificent Malika Jahan was choking on her own blood by the time he stopped raining blows on her face and every exposed part of her body with his fists and well-shod feet. He took savage pleasure in the knowledge that none of her devious arts could restore her damaged face and form now. But to her credit, she did not cry out once.

When he was done, the guards clapped his wife in chains and led her away. A few months in the dungeon would sweeten her disposition and hopefully usher her to an early grave. Unlike her father, she certainly did not deserve the mercy of a quick, clean death. Her eyes were swollen nearly shut, but Alauddin was gratified to note that they were burning over with hate. And more importantly, grudging respect. It was without doubt the sweetest moment of his life.

1

Summons from the King

The girl was singing beside her favourite lily pond, feeding the fish bits of unleavened bread. She tended to do that sort of thing often since the little lady was something of a dreamer.

Her parents watched their daughter, a vision in her gold brocade ghagra and emerald-green choli. The princess's attendants liked few things better than dressing up their extraordinarily beautiful charge and saw no reason to stint on their efforts, even if she was asleep in her chambers or merely pottering about in the garden. They had arranged her hair artfully and outlined her eyes with kohl. Her natural complexion was so fine and flawless, it was an ornament in itself. Beauty like hers needed no enhancement, they would say fondly, even as they devoted themselves wholeheartedly towards improving on the gifts the Creator had so generously bestowed on her.

Be it at the end of a long day spent in study (her mother had insisted, confident that her daughter would some day be a queen and deciding it would not do if she were unlettered), or riding her mare, or simply nursing a nasty cold, the princess seemed incapable of looking anything but flawlessly beautiful. Even when she ignored her mother's strict instructions, which was often, and spent the day basking in the harsh sun or chasing after her pets, her clothes never became dirty. Her hair, which flowed in a cascade of glorious waves all the way to the small of her back, seldom looked messy. The same exertions which soaked her friends and cousins in a layer of unbecoming perspiration and grime, somehow gave her translucent skin a certain lustre, leaving her aglow with radiance.

'Padmavati grows more beautiful by the day . . .' Mahisamara beamed.

Leelavati nodded. 'Her beauty will stand her in good stead of course, but since I am the one bringing her up, she will also have many talents to draw upon when she is a queen.'

She will have many talents to draw upon, despite your best efforts, Mahisamara amended. But since he was a prudent man, he did not say the words aloud. However, his wife's frown indicated that she had heard them anyway. He did not understand how the woman was privy to his innermost thoughts.

They were standing on the terrace that overlooked the charming garden below, bursting with rare flowering plants and creepers, ornamental shrubs and fruit trees – the result of the princess's personal undertaking. She had decorated the wooden enclosure surrounding her quarters in the harem with paintings done in vegetable dyes, made for her by a maid who had learnt the art when she had worked under Jain monks.

The paintings depicted riotous scenes of dancing apsaras, musicians, gods and goddesses, flowers, fish and birds in a profusion of bright colours. Her winged friends resided in spacious constructions woven with cane, fronds of palm and even fine muslin cloth. And she had managed to persuade her mother to allow her to raise lambs, chickens, stray puppies and even a few rabbits – a gift from a passing mendicant. The last were testing Leelavati's patience with their alarming promiscuity and the speed at which they bred.

Padmavati was still singing. She had a lovely lilting voice which soared with youthful exuberance and conveyed an ocean of passionate feeling. And as was usually the case, everybody in the vicinity paused in the middle of whatever they were doing to listen to her songs.

The princess was their only child. In the past, Leelavati had given birth to five stillborn boys. The jyotishis they had consulted said that Padma, as she was affectionately called, was special, blessed with the spirit of Durga Mata herself. No one had expected her to survive but she had proved them wrong. Clearly, she had imbibed the strength of her fallen brothers and been marked by destiny to turn the tide of history.

Leelavati believed them. Yes, she had harangued her husband into greasing their palms with gold and silver before their visit to prevent them from predicting ill omens. But it had been a wise precaution. Their bribe had ensured that the priests refrained from using words such as inauspicious when preparing her chart. The very word could destroy their daughter's life and mar her future irrevocably. Leelavati knew one too many girls blessed with looks comparable to Padma's, who had failed to make a good match because of unfavourable horoscopes. These girls usually went mad from the enforced celibacy, became bitter and plain, or eventually killed themselves. It was better to be poor and ugly than inauspicious.

It was why Leelavati had insisted they leave nothing to chance. But despite the bribe, she was still convinced the jyotishis had spoken the truth.

As Padma grew up, her family's prospects were enhanced a hundredfold because she blossomed into such an enchanting girl. No one could resist her charms. They belonged to the illustrious line of the Chauhans of Jalore and enjoyed the favour of their king, Kanhadadeva. Still, there was no denying that their power and influence was not what it could have been.

Mahisamara was Maharaj Kanhadadeva's nephew. He was that rare kind of man who got on well with everybody because he did not have an ambitious or envious bone in his body, was loyal to a fault and was always competent without ever aspiring towards brilliance. In fact, he even got along with his elder brother, Sthaladeva, to whom Maharaj Kanhadadeva had entrusted the principality of Siwana, which was where they lived.

Sthaladeva was a fine warrior and a principled ruler, whose gruff exterior failed to mask the genuine affection he bore towards his younger brother. It was a bond that had survived even the bitter animosity between their principal wives, who hated the very sight of each other.

Despite this, Sthaladeva always treated his brother's wife with respect, openly admired her keen political acumen and positively doted on Padma, making time in his busy schedule to visit her, always armed with presents, denying her nothing. Even his wife, the odious Saraswati, who never let people forget she had borne her husband a son, Pratap, had often said that Padma may have received her looks from the Creator but her noble heart and warmth of character, she inherited from her father. The jibe was supposed to rub salt in a festering wound.

Leelavati had never been particularly good-looking. She was fully fleshed and somewhat portly, even though she ate sparingly unless she was angry at the world, which was most of the time, in which case she took to consuming prodigious quantities of rabadi. Her stubborn features were further marred by dull, dead eyes and excessively large, fleshy lips which when parted, revealed crooked and stained teeth.

Leelavati did not mind in the least when people commented on her unattractiveness. She was content with the brilliant mind and the indomitable spirit within her unflattering exterior. Besides, she knew Padma had inherited the same traits in addition to her courage and wit. In fact, it pleased her no end that her daughter's intelligence, unlike her own, was intuitive without being calculative. Most people were so taken with Padma's charm and grace that her sharp mind almost always took them by surprise.

Padma started winning hearts early. Marriage proposals had begun to pour in even when she was still a pudgy toddler. People would insist on petting her, cooing over her lush ringlets and abundant lashes. Even then people had been enraptured both by her radiant smile as well as her howling fits! Sthaladeva would ignore Saraswati's express disapproval and hold little Padma on his knee while conferring with his ministers or entertaining visiting dignitaries, and she would sit there quiet as a mouse or amuse herself by tugging at his beard to see if he would squeal.

Now they were flooded with requests for her hand and Leelavati was determined that her daughter would only wed the most powerful sovereign in the land. No one had met her exacting standards so far. Perhaps her daughter was fated to marry an emperor in a far-off land, who would bring the entire world under his yoke. How she would bask in the reflected glory then!

'My brother and I will be leaving within the hour for Jalore.' Her husband interrupted her reverie. 'Jajjadeva will be there as well.'

Mahisamara had received a summons from Maharaj Kanhadadeva. His instructions had been explicit – the matter was of utmost importance and they were to make haste. He knew Leelavati wouldn't be happy at all. She had never forgiven Kanhadadeva for favouring Sthaladeva over her husband.

Well aware that her husband feared her silence every bit as much as he feared her caustic tongue, Leelavati said nothing.

'Maharaj Kanhadadeva probably wishes to discuss a suitable alliance for our Padma,' Mahisamara said with forced eagerness. 'He has always wanted a daughter but all he ever got were boisterous boys who came into this world determined to raise hell. It is why he treats Padma like his own daughter.'

'I highly doubt that,' Leelavati retorted sharply. 'This meeting is most likely about the situation in Delhi. Jalaluddin is dead, I am told. Murdered by his nephew! Didn't I predict that old Greybeard would come to a bad end after what he did to Balban's descendants? Not that the Delhi sultans were paragons of virtue, mind you ... The Mamluk slaves and pleasure boys of that monster, Muhammad of Ghur, who dared call themselves sultans, fully deserved the tragic fate that befell them. Now there will be a war for succession between Jalaluddin's sons and Alauddin.'

Mahisamara had hoped Jalaluddin would have a long reign. For a veteran soldier, the old shah had been a man of peace who preferred not shedding any blood and showed unheard-of clemency when it came to his foes. Unlike his predecessors, he had little interest in the business of war or in amassing vast treasure, slaves and women.

'Maharaj Kanhadadeva probably wants to take advantage of the situation,' Leelavati predicted. 'Be sure to tell him that I would appreciate it if he did not use my daughter as a pawn in his ineffectual power games!'

Of course, it is only your prerogative to use my little girl

19

to further your boundless ambition, Mahisamara mused to himself. He knew of his wife's grandiose plans when it came to their daughter. In her opinion, the ideal husband for Padma would be an all-conquering warrior king. Of course, the other important prerequisite was that the groom prove himself malleable to Leelavati's will.

Mahisamara had entirely different notions of a suitable groom. And Padma had very clear views on the subject too.

'I'd rather not get married at all,' she had told them. 'Why should I go to a strange man's house when I am happy exactly where I am? Why can't I stay right here with the two of you and all my friends?'

He had expected Leelavati to slap her senseless but his wife's only weakness was their daughter, and in a practically unheard-of occurrence, she had deigned to smile and had actually bothered to explain. 'I too felt the same way when I was your age but if my mother had listened, instead of caning me to within an inch of my life, there would be no one to take care of your father, whose enemies would have cheerfully left his head for the crows, and you yourself wouldn't have been born.'

Padma had looked a bit solemn and Leelavati had added, 'However, when you are queen, you could change the laws of the land and make it a criminal offence to make a girl do something against her will. For all that to happen, you have to be clever and do exactly as your mother tells you.'

'When I become queen, I will make it unlawful for mothers to tell their daughters exactly what to do!' had been the young girl's cheeky reply, and before Leelavati could smack her for impertinence as well as testing the limits of her patience, she had fled. Mahisamara could have sworn Leelavati had deliberately let their daughter escape, and for that alone, he would have forgiven his wife her many sins in this life, the ones that had preceded it and future ones too.

Padma's song had drawn to a close and, sensing their gaze upon her, she turned to bestow a brilliant smile on her parents. Mahisamara felt his heart seize up with love for this impossibly fragile-looking girl, who had brought so much joy into his life.

At that moment, all Mahisamara wanted was for Padma to remain his little girl so he could protect her for all of eternity from every hurt, disappointment and pain the fates showered all mortals with. If the gods saw fit to grant him a boon, he would have asked that they preserve the perfect happiness of her youth and keep her safe from baleful influences and the evil eye. He hoped the gods were listening.

'Keep your wits about you!' Leelavati cut in. 'You will need them for this top-secret meeting with Kanhadadeva and Jajjadeva. And don't you worry about Padma. Remember what the jyotishis said? They had never seen a horoscope like hers. Wherever she goes in this dark world, she will brighten it with her mere presence, spreading prosperity and happiness like Goddess Lakshmi herself. Now go!'

It was only after he had shuffled out that Leelavati closed her eyes and added her own prayers to her husband's, fully convinced the gods were more likely to listen to her. 'Let only the one who is truly worthy of my Padma take her hand in marriage! Keep her safe and shelter her from the troubles of this miserable existence!'

2

The Omen

Padma had insisted on accompanying Mahisamara and her Uncle Sthaladeva to Jalore. Her cousin and best friend Pratap was also not one to be left behind. Leelavati had put up a token resistance before allowing herself to give in. She knew her daughter's mind too well and had already made arrangements for the girl to accompany her father and his brother. It was important that she travel a bit and get an idea about how to carry herself with grace and dignity in unfamiliar surroundings. Besides, her daughter would be married soon and she had no wish to deny her anything.

Leelavati had a word with her brother-in-law before their departure. Sthaladeva was taller than Mahisamara. Barring that, both men were almost identically handsome, with the same broad shoulders and hardened physique of seasoned warriors. Yet, Sthaladeva had a certain intensity and effortless regal presence, which ensured that people took him seriously, as opposed to how they tended to ignore his younger brother.

One of the reasons his wife Saraswati hated Leelavati so much was that Sthaladeva often discussed affairs of the state with her.

'Delhi is in a state of uproar!' Sthaladeva began without preamble. 'I was just listening to the reports. The information we have received so far is inadequate and contradictory but only one thing is certain: Jalaluddin is dead by Alauddin's hand. I will know more about it after conversing with Maharaj Kanhadadeva at Jalore. But, here I admit, you were right! Greybeard, as you called him, certainly did not last long! A mere six years . . .'

He removed his ruby-encrusted gold ring and handed it to her. He had lost the wager they made the last time they had discussed the happenings in Delhi. Leelavati accepted it with a gracious smile.

'It is very kind of you to remember, Sire, but may I remind you that another prediction was made at the time? Regarding who would hold the reins of power in Delhi, which you insisted was most unlikely.'

Sthaladeva's eyes twinkled. 'I should have known better than to question your judgement. My brother and I allowed hope to blind us. We wanted peace with the invaders and even the possibility of an understanding with the shah. Jalaluddin, with his pacifist approach, would certainly have seen eye to eye with us. They say he wept when he reached Delhi and saw what had happened to Balban's line. Although he certainly had a hand in the wanton destruction. In fact, he felt it would be disrespectful to sit on his sultan's throne and so he ruled from Kilughari instead. With him at the helm, the dogs of war would have ceased their infernal barking. The respite would have helped strengthen our position considerably. Alas, it was not to be!'

'Your vision is a laudable one,' Leelavati said impatiently, 'but it was never going to come to fruition, given that you and your brother constitute a minority. The hotheads, on our side as well as theirs, will never be happy unless they are making war. See what happened to poor Greybeard when he went against the tide? The old shah turned back from the siege of Ranthambore saying he did not want his men and fellow Muslims dying on his account, but his actions were construed as a sign of cowardice. Alauddin Khalji will not make the same mistake, mark my words!'

'I think my emerald ring will remain safely in my possession,' Sthaladeva scoffed, as Mahisamara joined them. 'I don't see how you can be so certain that it is Alauddin who will sit on the throne of Delhi. Jalaluddin is survived by a brood of bloodthirsty sons who will not let his treachery go unpunished. Arkali Khan, his eldest, has already proved his mettle during Malik Chajju's rebellion. As Balban's nephew, stationed at Kara, Chajju insisted the throne was his and Hatim Khan, the governor of Oudh, joined him, do you remember? They are fortunate Jalaluddin spared their lives. His courtiers were dumbfounded at this show of mercy towards a rival.'

'At least he had the sense to punish the traitors and confiscate Kara as well as Oudh!' Sthaladeva shook his head in disbelief. 'Incidentally, both were given to Alauddin for his exemplary role in the conquest of Malwar and Bhilsa. As for Arkali Khan, he is a fine warrior and showed the stuff he was made of when he recaptured Mandawar from the Rajputs and repelled the Mongol hordes.'

Mahisamara nodded. 'Even though Alauddin has established himself as a fearsome warrior, they say that the man has no control over his own harem. That his wife and his mother-in-law order him about as if he were a slave, and never lose an opportunity to belittle him–'

He would have gone on but Leelavati shot him a glare before cutting him off. 'Those women are fools! They should've poisoned Alauddin or got an assassin to do the job. Instead, all they have done is pricked and jabbed repeatedly at his ego, leaving it stricken and bleeding. There is no animal as dangerous as a wounded one. He will lash out at all and sundry, leaving a trail of death, destruction and pain, enough to mirror his own. Thousands will pay the price for their hauteur. My dear mother always said it takes a woman to make or break a man! As for Arkali Khan, he is currently stationed in Multan, and may I point out that it is a long way from Delhi unlike Kara.'

The brothers exchanged uneasy glances. Leelavati had drawn up a disturbing vision of the future and they could only hope she was wrong.

'The Chauhans have fought worse enemies in the past and even if they did not live to tell the tale, they are survived by valiant descendants who have hopefully learned about turning disaster into triumph.' Leelavati ended the pregnant pause. 'What are you waiting for? Go! And may the gods be with you!'

Leelavati performed the aarti herself, pleased that her intolerable sister-in-law was indisposed. Saraswati was usually suffering from some odious bodily ailment or the other, exclusive to chronically lazy people. But it was all for the best. No man must be forced to endure having to look at her repulsive mien at the onset of a journey, especially one as crucial as this one.

She held the gold thali as the men lowered their hands over the flame and applied the tilak to their foreheads, murmuring a few words of blessing as she did so. To her husband and Padma, a series of quick instructions were given and to Sthaladeva, her voice was a mere whisper, 'I suggest you enjoy the emerald ring while it is still in your possession, Sire!'

She even had a smile for Pratap, who she was still unsure about, given that he was Saraswati's son. However, she had to admit the boy was fond of Padma and he had inherited his father's strength as well as nobility. But the trouble with the best of boys was that they grew up to be men and there was no saying how they would turn out.

As the procession wound its way out of the fort, Leelavati tried to still the anxiety in her heart. She frowned with displeasure as Padma leaped out of the palki which had been readied for her, and clambered atop her mare which Pratap was holding in place. For a brief moment, she wondered if she had not spoilt the child rotten. As the gate was raised, Leelavati murmured a prayer to the gods to keep them safe from harm.

When she opened her eyes, the sun was high in the sky, dazzling in its brightness. Suddenly a flock of pigeons took wing, soaring towards the golden orb. It was too late when they saw the dark speck swooping towards them. The strike was quick and deadly. There was a burst of feathers and amid the panicked cooing of the birds and the eagle's own harsh cries, two carcasses fell to the ground, droplets of their blood glittering like rubies as the light caught them.

Leelavati did not think of herself as a superstitious person but she shivered. Why would an eagle make two strikes but leave its prey behind without carrying it away safely secured in its talons? It had to be an omen and not a particularly fortuitous one. Were her husband and Sthaladeva in danger? And what about Padma?

As much as Leelavati tried to reassure herself, there was no getting away from the sinking feeling of doom that had turned her blood to ice.

3

To Jalore

'You are afraid I will win,' Padma said in a huff. 'I always win against Father, ask him! And Pratap as well, though he'll never admit it! And if you are going to be difficult, I will not tell you what I know . . .'

The journey across the undulating plains and occasional wooded areas and hillocks that sprouted up without warning was enlivened considerably thanks to Padma, who rode her mare alongside the two men and her cousin for the entire duration.

To their jaded eyes, the landscape could not be more commonplace but, as far as the princess was concerned, it was entirely magical. Of course, this journey was even more colourful because Padma kept up an incessant chatter. Presently, she was annoyed because her uncle had refused to allow her to prod her mare into a gallop so they could see who would reach Jalore first.

'Well, what do you know?' Sthaladeva asked.

'It is important and not even Mother knows about it!' she said.

The brothers glanced at each other.

'Is it about the man you are going to marry?' Sthaladeva teased gently.

'Of course it is!' Pratap chimed in. 'I am told he has a paunch, wobbly thighs and is bald. What's more, his double chin has a triple chin!' Pratap doubled over with laughter. 'The only thing he is good at is eating, and so naturally he belches all the time. But apparently that is not as bad as his flatulence problem. To his credit though, he has crushed many an enemy beneath his bulk. He is the hero my aunt has been searching high and low for, anxious to get rid of her pest of a daughter! He is the ideal match for Padma here, with her truly hideous looks and horrible behaviour! No wonder her mother is trying her best to give her away!'

'I dare you to say that in front of my mother!' Padma retorted, frowning at her cousin who was still shaking with laughter. Her father and uncle were too dignified to laugh outright at his juvenile humour but they were having a difficult time suppressing their smiles.

'It is about the secret meeting that is to take place at Jalore ...' she began theatrically, waiting till their attention was focused entirely on her.

'How would you know that?' Mahisamara queried.

'Well, I visited the slave quarters earlier today to get some paints and see if someone would help me smuggle some sweets out of the kitchen, and I heard something ... You know, they talk freely in my presence because they think I am too young to comprehend. In their eyes, I'll always be a little girl! But Mother always says it never hurts to be well informed. The things I could tell you ...' Her smile was ghoulish.

Sthaladeva wasn't surprised. They believed that a woman's sensibility was far too delicate for blood and gore, or coarse, obscene humour, but he had noticed that during festivals or while dignitaries were being entertained, the women behind the curtained enclosures had a far bigger appetite for violence and ribaldry than men. There were times when he couldn't help thinking that had the women been put in charge of their armies, none of the foreign invaders would have dared set foot on their land.

'So what *did* you hear?' he asked his niece.

'I heard that Maharaj Kanhadadeva is planning an alliance of the sort Prithviraj Chauhan had forged against Muhammad of Ghur in the first battle of Tarain,' said Padma. 'He wants Mewar, Jalore, Ranthambore and possibly even Gujarat to make a pact and present a united front, in the hope that the other thirty-six Rajput clans will fall in.' She looked so pleased with herself at the breadth of her knowledge and grasp of things that Sthaladeva reached out and patted her head.

Sthaladeva had suspected as much himself, but was amazed by the vastness of his uncle's ambition. It was commendable he sought to unite the warring factions, but that sort of thing was easier said than done, given that their world was known to revolve on the will and small-mindedness of weak men. Similar attempts in the past had come to naught over the smallest of issues.

'It is an ambitious project, I'll give Maharaj Kanhadadeva that! And I am sure he is perfectly capable of seeing such a vast undertaking to fruition,' said Mahisamara, ever the optimist.

Padma nodded. Beside her, Pratap looked bored. He was not one for long-winded discussions; he preferred to be in the thick of action.

'Perhaps the Maharaj's effort will pay off but I doubt it,' Sthaladeva replied. 'Hammira Chauhan of Ranthambore is a direct descendant of Prithviraj Chauhan III and there is no doubt he is every bit as proud and reckless as his ancestor. I fear he will insist on leading such a coalition, even though in my opinion, Maharaj Kanhadadeva is more suitable, being his elder and a far more experienced statesman. We are Chauhans too but they have always treated us like members of an inferior branch.

'As for young Ratan Singh of Chittor, he has only recently succeeded his father Samar Singh. The Rawals belong to the Guhilot line, claiming descent from Lord Rama himself. Ratan Singh would certainly feel it is his God-given right to take charge of this expedition. Don't even get me started on the other clans and factions that make up the rest of the Rajputs!'

Padma was taken aback by the cynicism and hopelessness that had crept into her uncle's voice but she wasn't having any of it. 'It need not be so bad, Uncle! Besides, you don't know for certain that Hammira and this Ratan Singh are going to be pig-headed. Who knows. Perhaps they will turn out to be delightful and every bit as accommodating as necessary.

'And so what if our people fight among ourselves? We have a far greater capacity for friendship and courage. And why limit ourselves to our own people for this coalition? Our land has always been a diverse one ... We could find a way to unite everyone irrespective of the language they speak or the religion they follow. It will not be easy but it is worth pursuing if we truly wish to usher in an age of peace and prosperity.'

Her eyes were shining with earnestness, and for a moment, Sthaladeva prayed that her impossible dream would some day come true. He glanced across at his brother and he knew Mahisamara felt the same way.

'You are a great one for talking!' Pratap butted in, sensing his father's mood had taken a turn for the worse, and annoyed that they insisted on discussing politics. 'It is very easy to assume you have all the answers, when in fact, you spend your days plaiting those rat tails you call hair and singing stupid songs in that voice which sounds like the squawking of crows! What would you know about a man's business?'

'I know I will be far better at it than you will ever be!' Padma was incensed. 'Especially since you are never going to be anything but a rogue and a lout. Wait and watch, in the future people will tell stories about the brave Queen Padmavati! As for you, the name Pratap the Pig will be whispered to terrify children about what happens to people who do nothing but eat, sleep and be excessively stupid!'

The cousins bickered through the rest of the journey, even during stops for rest and refreshment, while Sthaladeva and Mahisamara pondered over their thoughts in silence. It was only when they approached Jalore Fort that they stopped fighting and promptly forget their differences.

The grandeur of the fort far outshone their home at Siwana. Perched high above the surrounding plains, the fort stood shoulder to shoulder with the majestic Aravalli range. Built entirely of stone that had been neatly cut and assembled by the best builders and artisans in the land, it was an impressive edifice. The walls were thick and high, almost entirely impervious to the attacks of enemies. Awed by the spectacle, they gaped in wonder, entering the fort in silence.

Maharaj Kanhadadeva rode out to meet them with his son, Virama, and his brother, Maladeva. All his courtiers were present and he welcomed his nephews with great fanfare. Sthaladeva and Mahisamara paid obeisance to the king who in turn embraced them warmly. In an age where treachery was all around, loyal men were hard to find, and the king was happy that his sister's sons did her memory proud.

His attention was immediately drawn to the princess, who was looking at him with frank curiosity from beneath her thick lashes. He had last seen Padmavati when she was a squalling infant, wrinkled and red as a monkey. How lovely she had grown! He was pleased to note that the poised young lady was not overwhelmed by the august company. And he was disarmed by that dazzling smile of hers which lit up her magnificent eyes.

The king of Jalore addressed a few words to Padmavati and within minutes they were chatting like old friends. Kanhadadeva was utterly charmed. Never before had he encountered such loveliness and good conduct among women! Pratap was stiff when presented to the king but later, Padma informed him that he had conducted himself with more aplomb than she had thought him capable of.

The townspeople had gathered for a view of the royal procession as it wound its way towards the palace, and called out their greetings to the king and his courtiers. Soon, it became apparent that Padmavati was the cynosure of all eyes, and the more enthusiastic folks in the crowds showered her with flowers, comparing her to Goddess Lakshmi. The adulation did not unsettle Padma, nor did she shrink from it; she merely accepted it with a gracious smile.

Maharaj Kanhadadeva took note of the girl's conduct and was satisfied. He had chosen well, and if all went according to plan, she would be key to fulfilling his vision for a glorious future that would eject the barbaric Muhammadans once and for all from Aryavarta.

~

Padma gasped with wonder when they were led into the Rudaladevi Palace. She had never seen such grandeur before. Her eyes drank in the luxuriously appointed apartments, the marble baths, gardens, little lotus ponds with multicoloured fish, courtyards and trellised walkways. Everything was bright, beautiful and polished to a high sheen. It reminded her of the stories she had heard about Amaravati – the fabled city of the gods.

Maharani Trinetra, looking resplendent in a chanderi sari worn with a blouse heavily embroidered in silver thread, awaited them there. Adorned with silver filigree jewellery, the grand matriarch welcomed her guests. Her ornaments complemented the flashes of lustrous white in her hair. She held the traditional engraved gold thali with a lamp and camphor for the aarti. Padma took copious mental notes, knowing that her mother and the other ladies back at Siwana would love all the details.

To her husband's surprise, Maharani Trinetra took the girl under her wing at once. Usually, she unequivocally abhorred anybody whose attractiveness rivalled hers. But she seemed willing to make an exception in this case even though Padmavati's looks were likely to eclipse the beauty of the apsaras themselves.

Padma would have liked to join the men but she allowed herself to be taken in hand by the maharani and led to the ladies' chambers. She supposed she would be expected to freshen up, partake of a meal, answer a whole lot of tedious questions, and rest. Fortunately, the maharani seemed kind, and who knew. Perhaps she would be like her mother and know more about the happenings at secret meetings than the men who held them.

Pratap couldn't resist throwing Padma a pitying glance as he left with Sthaladeva and Mahisamara. They too would rest awhile before their private audience with the king. In all likelihood, there would be plenty of entertainment and revelry later. He knew Padma was annoyed about not being able to join them, but she was too much of a lady to stick out her tongue at him.

4

The Plans of Kings

'The news from Delhi is not good!' Maharaj Kanhadadeva began without preamble.

He was treating their meeting like an emergency session. The presence of Jajjadeva, legendary general of Maharaj Hammira Chauhan, lent considerable weight to the proceedings. He cut an impressive figure with his ponderous manner and stately appearance. The great warrior was almost forty years old but his hair was still dense and unmarked with grey. Though he held himself still, his eyes darted about with predatory energy.

The brothers watched the old general surreptitiously. Jajjadeva seemed to be hewn from granite, and by their reckoning, wouldn't yield an inch once he took a stand. Although he was courteous, it didn't make him any less formidable.

Maharaj Kanhadadeva was less intimidating, but that was because he was their uncle. He was a smallish man who no longer possessed a flat, hard belly or a full head of hair. Yet, he had a stentorian voice and a roar that could rally his men in the heat of battle and strike fear into his enemy's hearts.

Among the Rajputs who prized warlike attributes over all else, Kanhadadeva was a legend. And it wasn't just because of his valour on the battlefield. Kanhadadeva's sainted father, Samanta Simha, had lived out his entire life, dying of natural causes at the end. Kanhadadeva had been perfectly content to serve under his father and king. Such patience and filial affection was a rare quality in these times. Too many princes grew tired of waiting for the throne and committed patricide with unbecoming alacrity.

His brother Maladeva was helping himself liberally to the food and drink. Even though he was a hearty eater and prodigious drinker, Maladeva was a small, compact man who looked more like a trader than a warrior. Between mouthfuls of roasted quail and beans, he observed his companions with watery eyes.

'As you know, Jalaluddin is dead!' the king continued, pausing to wet his throat with some water. He was also famously abstemious.

'Murdered more like!' Jajjadeva clarified. 'Killed

treacherously by his nephew and son-in-law, the notorious Alauddin, formerly governor of Kara.'

'I am told the shah's head is being carried to Delhi and Alauddin has won over most of the courtiers by distributing his ill-gotten gains with outright profligacy. They are firing gold coins at the gathered crowds with a manjanik. The good citizens who were originally baying for his blood are now calling him their deliverer! Fools!'

'What about his sons?' Sthaladeva asked as he removed his emerald ring and twisted it absently between his fingers. 'Surely Arkali Khan will avenge his father's death and claim the throne for himself? They say he is an able warrior. In all probability, he has already assembled his troops at Multan and is marching towards Delhi even as we speak.'

'That is what a sensible man would do . . .' Jajjadeva responded drily, 'but some of these princes are born with addled brains. Of course, I blame the mothers for this. When she heard the news, Jalaluddin's wife panicked and placed her youngest son, Khader Khan, on the throne. She then sent messengers to Arkali Khan, urging him to hasten back to Delhi. The thickheaded prince, however, was deeply offended that his mother had declared Khader as the shah, so he continues to sulk behind the walls of his fortress in Multan. Now both his mother and brother have been imprisoned. We can be certain Khader Khan has been blinded if not killed outright. Alauddin's brother, Ulugh Khan, has been dispatched with a strong army to Multan. The Khan's orders are to return with the head of Jalaluddin's surviving son mounted on a spear.'

'That is not all . . .' Kanhadadeva grunted. 'This monster, who is currently the greatest threat to our sovereignty, is only getting started. His successful plunder of Devagiri has merely whetted his appetite for more. There is news that he plans to declare a holy war . . . what do they call it?'

'Jihad . . .' Mahisamara's voice was filled with dread. So much for ushering in a new era of peace! The last thing they needed was another fanatic like Mahmud of Ghazni or Muhammad of Ghur. The Rajputs hadn't fared well with their likes, even though the bards had done a remarkable job of glorifying their ignoble defeat at the hands of foreign invaders, presenting it as a stirring example of valour.

'She was right!' Sthaladeva muttered under his breath, thinking of Leelavati's words. 'Alauddin is dangerous. Men will follow a supreme commander who has repeatedly proven himself to be successful and promises treasures beyond their wildest dreams.'

They really had their work cut out for them this time around, thought Sthaladeva. For starters, they would need better intelligence and reliable spies to permeate every branch of Alauddin's administration, army and household. It was important that they knew the mind of the man they sought to defeat. And defeat Alauddin they must, or they would risk having him conquer their lands, annihilate their people and everything else they held dear. Conventional warfare would be inadequate to beat this new tyrant. But how was he going to convince Maharaj Kanhadadeva of all this?

'Of course, this new shah must be stopped!' said Maharaj Kanhadadeva. 'We will join forces against the Muhammadan menace. The Chauhans of Jalore and Ranthambore as well as the Guhilots of Mewar will be the backbone of a new Rajput confederacy, the likes of which has never been seen before. We will send emissaries to the rajas of Marwar, Bundi, Malwa, Ujjain ... We will counter their jihad with a dharmayuddha! Together we will give the shah a taste of might and valour of the sort he has never experienced before! His followers will be driven back to the same God who sends them here to make a nuisance of themselves!'

Sthaladeva was as religious as the next man, but he was a warrior first. Why did politicians conflate the two? The Muslims believed that dying in a battle waged for their faith would gain them instant access to heaven and an eternity in the arms of their houris – the beautiful virgins of paradise, while the Hindus believed in the endless cycle of birth and death. When it came to war, the former seemed a more promising prize to soldiers. How was he going to get his men to win battles when the Hindu afterlife offered nothing tantalizing for ordinary men? Besides, big speeches made him nervous. Words seldom won battles, but they could certainly trigger them.

All through the king's heroic declaration, Maladeva continued to eat. Jajjadeva was non-committal. Sthaladeva and Mahisamara were not sure how to respond. In fact, Sthaladeva had never felt so restless and uneasy before.

'May I speak frankly, Maharaj?' Sthaladeva finally spoke up.

His uncle nodded, even though he wasn't happy about his nephew's request. As king, all he wanted from his nephews was blind obedience, not their opinions. Still, he allowed him to speak his mind.

'I agree we must join forces with every Rajput clan, Your Highness,' Sthaladeva began. 'However, after making the pact, we all stay safely inside our individual fortresses, and when members of the coalition are under attack, it is not possible to send help in time or in sufficient numbers to make a difference. I suggest we unite and take the initiative to attack this time! Alauddin has yet to consolidate his position. We must strike hard and fast at the very heart of Delhi and seize power.

'But we cannot stop there. We must bring the Deccan and the lands to the south under your hegemony, using overtures of friendship wherever possible and force when needed. Nobody can doubt or question our worth as warriors; we have proven ourselves time and again, and at great cost to ourselves. Now, it is vital that the length and breadth of this land be brought under a single ruler so we can present a united front against foreign invaders and repel them once and for all.'

Maharaj Kanhadadeva was taken aback by his nephew's impassioned speech. Talk of still waters running deep!

As for Jajjadeva, he was fed up with these youngsters who thought the world of themselves and proposed new-fangled ideas guaranteed to get all of them slaughtered like chickens! Maladeva chose that moment to belch loudly, conveying his contempt.

Sthaladeva was already regretting his decision to speak up. He suspected that if his words were taken out of context, they would think he was ambitious. And ambitiousness was often indicative of a scheming, treacherous mind.

Had Sthaladeva just dared to suggest that their political strategies were inadequate? Mahisamara wondered if his brother had gone too far. Maharaj Kanhadadeva and Jajjadeva were both traditionalists. To suggest such a radical departure from convention could be treason.

Mahisamara was planning to salvage the situation by rephrasing his brother's radical notions in a manner that would be more palatable, but he wasn't prepared for the words that spilled forth from between his own heavily moustachioed lips. 'The Mongols who were forced to convert to Islam but are treated abominably by their fellow Muslims may share our interests. We can try to make them our allies and then Alauddin will have to rethink his strategy before declaring a holy war . . .'

Maharaj Kanhadadeva was mostly humane but he hated the Muslim invaders because of the destruction they caused to their people and lands. The invaders had persisted in their persecution of Hindus, although in all fairness, not all the sultans believed in enforcing such hate-filled policies. As a retaliatory measure, Maharaj Kanhadadeva thought the only way to deal with the aggressor was to be every bit as fanatical. Mahisamara knew this about his uncle and his ill-advised words were sure to make the king angry.

'I am going to pretend you did not suggest we join hands with those who have repeatedly dishonoured our most sacred beliefs. We are all human beings but we are not the same. A lion does not consort with a lowly rat, even though they are both animals.' The king took a deep breath and then continued, 'Jajjadeva has assured me that Maharaj Hammira Chauhan is amenable to forming a confederacy, which will serve as the bulwark against an enemy attack. We Chauhans must set the example for others.'

Jajjadeva nodded. Sthaladeva decided it was good to know that theoretically at least the Chauhans of Jalore and Ranthambore were willing to set aside their differences and forget the bitter acrimony of the past.

'Rawal Ratan Singh is a reasonable man. I have already sent him messengers offering the hand of one who is the pride of our clan so we may be united by the bond of a matrimonial alliance.'

Mahisamara tried to look away but the king had pinned him in place with his intense gaze.

'It pleases me to say he has agreed to take our Padmavati as his wife, and it will be a joyous occasion indeed when the nuptials are solemnized here in Jalore within the month.'

Sthaladeva hoped his own face did not mirror the dumbstruck expression on his brother's. They ought to have seen this coming. And now it was too late. The king had given his word and they were bound by the iron diktats of duty.

The brothers accepted their king's embrace, thanking him for his magnanimity, while Maladeva stopped eating for long enough to smirk at them. Jajjadeva remained inscrutable.

'This is a fortuitous match. May it be the beginning of a new, golden age!' Kanhadadeva pronounced before dismissing his audience.

5

The Suitable Groom

At the exact moment when her future was being decided, Padma was deep in conversation with Maharani Trinetra, whom she found fascinating. The maharani had a lot of interesting news about the decadence of the late Delhi Sultanate and more than a few outrageous scandals to share. Padma particularly enjoyed the stories about Balban's grandson, the late Sultan Kaiqubad, since they involved his ladies of pleasure who pranced half-naked through the streets of Delhi to the accompaniment of much music and merriment.

'They say Kaiqubad was stricken down by a nasty disease that left him paralysed and gibbering like an infected monkey!' the maharani told her with ghoulish relish. 'The diseased sultan's power-hungry courtiers placed his three-year-old son, Kayumas, on the throne, hoping to rule in his stead, but Jalaluddin Khalji, who had been one of Balban's generals, ordered his own sons to do the dirty work and rid the realm of both the imbecilic father and infant son, before appointing himself as the shah of Delhi. With the sultans gone, the shahs were poised to wreak havoc!'

As Padma sipped the delicious badam sheera, listening with bated breath, the maharani filled her in with all the gossip, including all the juicy details about the latest shah's capture of the Delhi throne. He seemed terrifying and Padma shivered involuntarily.

'Our spies tell us he is a peculiar man. After he ascended the throne, Alauddin rounded up everyone who had betrayed the old regime, confiscated their property and sentenced them to death. And these were the very same people he had bribed!' The maharani's brows twitched with amusement. 'Isn't it funny . . . how the traitor cannot abide fellow traitors?'

Padma, who was listening with rapt attention, ventured her opinion. 'I feel sorry for the poor man!' Seeing that her audience was taken aback, she hastened to clarify. 'People envy kings but what is the point of a crown and throne when it is accursed and stained with the blood of innocent people? The shah had his king, who was also his kin, murdered. Since he is treacherous, he cannot trust anyone. He assumes everyone will have the same character as him. His guilt will cast a gloomy pall over his reign. Everywhere he looks, he will see fear and revulsion. To add to that, there will always be people who will want him dead. He will never be at peace.'

'But power and gold will always be worth it . . .' the maharani insisted.

'To each his own.' Padma shrugged. 'I wonder how he can look his wife in the eye after murdering her father and imprisoning her mother!'

'Let us hope his wife does us all a favour and sticks a jewelled dagger into her husband's ribs while he sleeps!'

'Let us hope not, Maharani Ma!' Padma shuddered. 'I can't understand revenge. Remember Draupadi? She wanted to avenge her humiliation by bathing her hair in the blood of the man who had disrobed her. Surely water would have served the purpose just as well? Because of her obstinacy, not only Dushasana but her own sons, brother, father and countless others were killed as well!' Padma paused. 'But going back to the subject, if the Mongols keep the shah busy for the rest of his days, he will not have time to think about us Rajputs, which would be much appreciated.'

The maharani liked what she saw. Mahisamara's daughter had a good heart and was intelligent as well. It would have been nice if this beautiful young girl had been her child! The gods had blessed her with many sons and some had survived infancy, growing to manhood. Now they were all so preoccupied with their wives and concubines, they had no time for their mother. She wondered if she should bring up a certain delicate topic, the one her husband had discussed with the men.

'My dear, I'd like to know what you think of something ...' she began, offering Padma a spicy kachori. The girl was so slender! Didn't her mother know that men preferred curvaceous women so that they didn't feel like they were taking a prickly twig to bed? But her bosom showed promise, and she was the loveliest young girl the maharani had ever seen.

'You have probably heard of the young Rawal Ratan Singh of Chittor?'

'Yes, Maharani Ma,' Padma replied absent-mindedly as she accepted the treat.

'He is the direct descendant of Bappa Rawal and I am told he is even more heroic and twice as good-looking,' said the queen. 'More importantly, he is a refined man with none of the vices and debauched habits which one associates with a ruler who came to power so young. They say he is humble and respectful of his elders. What do you think about him?'

The maharani had never seen the Rawal or even interested herself in him until recently, but nevertheless, she was confident he was a decent and clean-cut young man. Whatever he was or wasn't, there was only one thing she was certain of – Rawal Ratan Singh was without a doubt the luckiest man in the world. She carefully studied Padma's face for a reaction.

Padma, who had bitten into a chilli, gasped and reached out for a sip of her sweet drink. When the heat in her cheeks had cooled, she replied, 'I am sure he is a wonderful man but why would I think of him? And Your Highness was going to tell me more about the new shah's somewhat complicated relationship with his wife and mother-in-law . . .'

Maharani Trinetra had been about to tell Padma a little something about the Rawal's somewhat complicated relationship with *his* first wife, Nagmati, but decided against it. It wouldn't be right to terrify the bride-to-be. Instead, she launched into a colourful anecdote about Malika Jahan, the new shah's wife, and her tendency to beat up his favourites in the harem.

Padma gasped in horror and the queen decided that even her dramatic flourishes were adorable. Once again, she couldn't help thinking that Rawal Ratan Singh was indeed very fortunate. This girl was special and any man with sense would know that a good wife was all he needed to make his way through the battlefield that was life. And the Creator simply did not make them more special than Padmavati of Siwana.

As for Padma, she had not been as distracted as she had led the maharani to believe when she had mentioned Rawal Ratan Singh. Hadn't her uncle mentioned him as well during their journey here? For reasons she could not understand, her heart beat a little faster when that particular name was mentioned.

A few days ago, she had known absolutely nothing about either Alauddin Khalji or Rawal Ratan Singh. But now they were all that was being discussed. A strange presentiment filled her being. She would have dwelt on what the fates had in store for her, but the maharani's maids had offered her a platter of milk sweets and Padma allowed herself to momentarily forget about the men who would soon be entwined with her own destiny.

6

A Royal Wedding

Maharaj Kanhadadeva was determined to spare no expense when it came to celebrating the match he had made possible. Their guests – the good folk of Chittor – would talk about this wedding for generations to come. They would remember the hospitality and generosity of the Chauhans of Jalore and treat Princess Padmavati with the love and respect she deserved. Leelavati had been annoyed by Kanhadadeva's decision to fix the match without her approval and conduct the wedding at Jalore instead of Siwana, but she forgave him when she saw the lavish preparations he had made.

'Rawal Ratan Singh is hardly an unsuitable match, but it would've been better if his domineering mother was already dead and his harridan of a first wife was out of the picture. A man surrounded by overbearing women is usually henpecked and if there is one thing I abhor above all else in a man, it is weakness,' she had confided to Sthaladeva. Discussing these issues with her sentimental husband was pointless.

'Even if Vishnu had taken an avatar for the express purpose of marrying our Padma, you would have still deemed him worthless!' Sthaladeva replied. 'Let us trust in the gods and hope for the best. People already treat her with the same reverence they reserve for Goddess Lakshmi. Wherever she goes, victory and prosperity are sure to follow!' he had consoled her.

In the days leading up to the wedding, Leelavati performed many arcane rituals daily to ward off the evil eye from Padma. She didn't want the fickle masses to raise her daughter on a pedestal. The only thing they liked more than a goddess was a fallen goddess to spew their hate on. And that was the last thing she wanted for her child.

The bridegroom and his party arrived a few weeks prior to the wedding and were accommodated in a separate palace that had been especially done up for the occasion. All the rooms were luxuriously appointed and provided with every amenity so the guests could relax in comfort after the endless wedding festivities and tedious rituals that the Brahmins insisted on performing. These included lengthy rites to call upon the gods to bless the union, cast aside baleful influences and do everything possible to bring about a balance in the seven combinations of doshas that could influence the future of both the bride and groom, and their extended families and respective kingdoms as well.

An army of servants, both male and female, hand-picked by the supervisors waited on the entire baraat, night and day. They indulged their every whim, no matter how outrageous, keeping the guests plied with food, drink and companions of their choice. There were musicians, dancers, acrobats, magicians and even a menagerie of trained animals to entertain them.

'It is unfair that the men get the most beautiful courtesans in the land to entertain them, while the women have to settle for annoyingly talkative parrots and monkeys jumping through hoops!' Maharani Trinetra complained to her husband, who shushed her in a manner she found most rude.

The men agreed that the highlight was a dance performance involving exotic snakes brought from a faraway land, which were bigger and more toxic than indigenous breeds. The gorgeous dancers were coy yet uninhibited as they performed the serpentine moves with sinuous grace, divesting their garments suggestively. The intoxicating spectacle, in tandem with wine, drove the men into a frenzy of orgiastic excitement.

Not to be left behind, the citizens of Jalore were more than happy to enter into the spirit of the celebrations, for they had already adopted Padmavati as their own. Thanks to the generosity of their king, food was distributed in large tents across the region and the people ate till their stomachs were bursting, blessing the couple with every mouthful. They poured into the temples and called down the blessings of the goddess on their beloved Princess Padmavati and her husband, the Rawal. In the evenings, every home was adorned with oil lamps and Jalore sparkled like the city of gods.

Cloth merchants, jewellers and florists did brisk business. Women cajoled their husbands to loosen their purse strings, swearing they did not have a piece of clothing or jewellery to wear for the momentous occasion. Tailors were kept busy, cutting yards and yards of fabric, sewing, making alterations, loosening or tightening waistbands, or embroidering cholis, chunnis and ghagras.

Mehendi artists were in high demand as many pairs of arms and feet had to be covered with intricate henna designs. This deprived the ladies the use of their limbs for a good portion of the day, which they used to their advantage by lazing and gossiping to their hearts' content. Children too were infected by this contagious enthusiasm and were in high spirits, getting underfoot and conducting raids into the kitchen to steal away large platters of sweetmeats and snacks.

In the middle of all this frenetic activity, Padmavati remained calm. She was cloistered in the inner reaches of the harem and so closely guarded that had she been inclined to pay attention to her immediate surroundings and situation, she would have felt like a prisoner.

The groom's female relatives visited her daily, bearing gifts, and Padmavati was displayed to them in the guise of every single one of the 1008 manifestations of Goddess Lakshmi. She was draped in yards of heavily embroidered and embellished fabric, enduring elaborate hairdos and wearing jewellery so heavy, an elephant would have collapsed under its weight. There were so many ceremonies, temple visits, rites and rituals that after a while she had no idea whether she was coming or going, and gradually sank into a dreamlike trance that made her look ethereal. All the women who beheld her sighed with envy.

No amount of discomfort or cheek-pinching disturbed her outward equanimity. She was the very epitome of charm. But deep down, Padma was anxious. Away from her home in Siwana, her gardens and pets, she felt marooned. The decision regarding her wedding had been taken so suddenly that she was still shocked by it. She may not even get a chance to say goodbye to her home and people.

There were moments during the day when she wished she could go back to simpler times, when she would tug playfully at her sleeping father's whiskers or lie on her mother's lap while enduring her stern admonitions regarding exemplary conduct. Pratap's ridiculous jokes. Uncle Sthaladeva's reassuring presence. Maids who gave her all the sweets she could eat and more. Grooms who had let her tend to the horses. She missed it all terribly.

Padma wondered if she would see Siwana again. Would it have been any easier to bear if she had been given a chance to bid farewell?

The days sped by and Padma never let her emotions show. On the night before the wedding, however, Leelavati awoke to find Padma curled up by her side. She had not done that in years.

The bride and groom were not allowed to see each other, of course, and Padma had not been remotely curious about the man she was going to marry. She had listened to all the stories his relatives had told her about Rawal Ratan Singh and smiled or laughed merrily on cue, but that was about it. Now, she was trembling with worry and there was only one person who could put her mind at ease.

'Are you awake?' she whispered to her mother, who sat up immediately.

Leelavati sent for glasses of warm milk with saffron sprinkled on top.

'What do you make of him, and please, won't you tell me the truth?' Padma asked, taking a sip of her drink.

'By all reports, he is a good man.' Leelavati was almost sure of it after scrutinizing the Rawal from afar and interrogating her husband and Sthaladeva mercilessly. 'And even if he isn't, it doesn't matter. I have taught you well. If you are patient and clever, you can mould him till he becomes the husband you want and deserve. Men and dogs aren't entirely dissimilar . . . they may have a natural inclination to bite and bark when rubbed the wrong way but if you are firm and establish that you are in charge, they tend to fall in line.'

Padma said nothing.

For the first and only time in her life, Leelavati was scared. For her daughter. She found herself dabbing her eyes every once in a while and was appalled at her weakness, making up for it by being even more short and brusque with everybody, especially her husband. Even during her own wedding to Mahisamara Leelavati had not shed a single tear. When her mother, overwhelmed by maternal affection, had hugged her daughter, Leelavati had remained unmoved. They had said that a stony-hearted bride like herself was a rarity, but that wasn't the truth either. Leelavati was proud, and she would rather die than show weakness in front of a whole township. It was how she intended to leave this world as well. Without undue sentiment or fanfare. Now, she hoped she had the right words to prepare her daughter for the journey that lay ahead.

Yes, Padma was a daydreamer but she was also a realist, and Leelavati didn't want to inflame her expectations with improbable visions of a perfect man and husband. That was the sort of foolishness that led to disappointment, followed by bitterness – the surest way to drive a man into a rival's waiting arms, or worse, erode a woman's looks. But then again, kings went astray even if their young wives were the most loving and devoted creatures who had nothing but a smile or kind word for them, not to mention the endless treats secreted within their ghagra-cholis.

Wives usually blamed the concubines. If their husbands had the services of countless experts in the art of love at their disposal, how could a good wife with no knowledge of bedroom antics, save her untrustworthy instincts, hope to compete? Of course, their men liked innocence and inexperience because it flattered their egos, but once the novelty wore off, they grew bored and started looking for pleasure elsewhere. A clever wife was one who learned to walk the fine line between goddess and whore.

Leelavati, however, did not mind the whores. They kept

her husband occupied and out of her hair, leaving her free to deal with bigger matters. And oddly, Leelavati's nonchalance ensured that Mahisamara was absolutely devoted to her, giving her precedence over his other wives and concubines. She found it annoying and hoped her daughter wouldn't assume that all men were like her father. Leelavati's silence prompted Padma to ask, 'How come you have nothing to say about my wedding night? And the nights to follow? Everybody keeps dropping these hints and there is innuendo enough to make a stone statue blush. Maharani Trinetra is more circumspect but she keeps advising me about how to keep my husband tied to my odhani long after the nuptials are concluded!'

'Of course, Maharani Trinetra would tell you all that,' Leelavati said in her crisp, disdainful tone. 'As for the wedding night, you already know about it from all the time you spend in the stables and the servant quarters. I know how you love gossip. Thanks to your Uncle Sthaladeva's ability to drive women mad, you have been exposed to more drama than is usual even in a harem. And of course, you follow my advice to be well informed most diligently. A more precocious brat I have yet to see! Even as a child you preferred to sit like a mouse in the company of adults, listening to all sorts of things that were not exactly appropriate for your age, but you got away with it, because you have always had the ability to look innocent when you are up to mischief. About the wedding night . . . it can only be experienced and not explained.'

'I knew you were not fooled but you usually let me stay . . .' Padma giggled. 'I am grateful. It was all very informative.'

'I am sure it was useful to listen to ladies wax eloquent about menstrual cramps, birthing, breastfeeding, the tricks to look young and the particulars about who was currently in the process of seducing whom. And let us not forget your innocuous presence in the slave quarters every time your kitten went "missing", just so you could stay updated on whatever dirt they had managed to dig up about our world! Pray, do tell what was so informative about all this?'

Padma took her time to get over her mirth before she framed a reply. 'From whatever I've heard, it seems there is not a single person in the harem who is completely happy. For instance, Tara wept for days because Uncle had stopped loving her and was besotted with her twin sister, Maya. Her distress upset her poor baby son who cried as well, until I played with him and made him stop. As for Maya, who had everything Tara wanted, Uncle was never enough because all she wanted was a child. In fact, she told me she wouldn't mind in the least even if the baby was a girl. I saw her cry too when she thought nobody was looking. As for Aunt Saraswati, she is Uncle's chief wife and the mother of his heir, and yet it seems to me she is unhappier than both of them put together . . .'

As Leelavati waited for her to continue, she topped up her milk from the silver glass.

'I learned that though pain is the reality and pleasure is the dream, in the end, they are both imposters. Happiness is a delusion too and it isn't right to expect anybody, even your husband, to serve it up to you on a silver platter . . .'

'Now you know what to do on your wedding night! Just repeat the exact same thing to your husband and you can both get a good night's sleep, which in the end is preferable to nocturnal acrobatics, if you ask me.'

'Who says I want to sleep on my wedding night?' Padma was a picture of wide-eyed innocence.

Seeing the look on her mother's face, Padma burst into an intense giggling fit. It was irresistible, and helplessly, Leelavati joined in. They laughed so hard and were so loud that they alarmed the maids who thought something terrible had happened.

~

The wedding was an event to remember. Looking resplendent in a traditional dhoti and kurta of gold cloth, a cummerbund, and a bejewelled red turban and ornamental jutis, the groom was the epitome of strength and dignity. He glanced meaningfully at the richly caparisoned elephants in red and gold like him and said, 'Thanks to the hospitality of Maharaj Kanhadadeva and my bride's family, I have eaten so well that the good folk of Jalore will be entirely forgiven if they were to confuse the groom with one of these pachyderms.'

The bride's party laughed uproariously. The anecdote was told and retold till it reached Padma's ears, making her laugh.

'I always wanted to marry someone who can make me laugh . . .' she confided in her mother, who said nothing.

The Rawal was good-natured, it was true, but Leelavati would have preferred a stronger man with a ruthless streak. At least he had somehow improved Padma's disposition, which counted for something.

Leelavati was sorry that people could not fully appreciate how gorgeous her daughter looked in her bridal finery, since her entire head and the better part of her face were covered by the aanchal. Those who had seen her, including Maharani Trinetra, had been moved to tears. Those present at the wedding went into raptures over the exquisite perfection of her form and features, as well as the graceful way she carried herself. The bride's family were fully satisfied with the spontaneous outpouring of love and affection for their beloved Padma.

Under a golden canopy, the couple performed the

sacred rites and rituals that would unite them in holy matrimony. The priests chanted solemn invocations to the gods to witness and bless the union. Generous amounts of ghee were poured into the flames and the plumes of smoke that rose ensured they were all choked up and teary-eyed.

Ratan was wiping his eyes, trying to ease the sting of the acrid fumes, when he caught his bride pretending to adjust her aanchal as she stole a glance at him. The mischievousness in her gaze melted his heart and the hustle and bustle of their wedding blurred till he was aware only of the gentle soul who was looking at him in silent adoration, unable to tear her gaze away from his.

Padma couldn't look away either as her heart danced with joy, delighted to have found the man of her dreams. She had not been prepared for how handsome and noble her husband looked. More importantly, his proximity made her feel warm and loved, even more so than her mother's lap. *He seems so kind*, she thought.

The chanting had risen to a crescendo as flower petals and gold coins were showered on the newly-weds. Neither of them was aware of what was happening around them. From that moment, everybody and everything they had ever known was swallowed up by the tidal wave of feelings that surged between their hearts. For evermore, it would be just the two of them.

7

The Coalition That Wasn't

Long after the wedding festivities were concluded, Maharaj Kanhadadeva was feeling expansive and insisted that Sthaladeva and Mahisamara dine and drink with him. Maladeva was snoring gently, his fingers loosely holding on to the near-empty goblet that had been his constant companion for the duration of the nuptials. He had amused himself by making ribald comments on the couple's wedding night, which Sthaladeva thought were in extremely bad taste.

'It was a beautiful ceremony . . .' Kanhadadeva reminisced. 'Our little princess does credit to us all. She is going to be the finest queen Aryavarta has seen, mark my words. People will remember her goodness long after we are no more and worship her memory.'

Moved by Maharaj Kanhadadeva's kindness, Mahisamara had tears in his eyes. Sthaladeva was proud of Padma too but mawkishness was not in his nature. Plus, there were some pressing issues that needed to be discussed immediately. Kanhadadeva had assured them that Hammira Chauhan would grace the wedding with his presence and later they could iron out the details regarding the ambitious coalition that would check Alauddin Khalji's advance. They needed to have a feasible plan of action to counter the shah who was becoming notorious for his sudden, swift strikes in unexpected places that were almost impossible to predict.

However, Hammira had not come. And neither had Jajjadeva. Sthaladeva was determined to have it out with his uncle, who continued to pretend that everything was going according to plan.

'Has there been any word from Hammira Chauhan?' he asked pointedly.

Maharaj Kanhadadeva looked at him reproachfully, but deigned to reply. 'Hammira, despite being a brave warrior, tends to be unreasonable on occasion.' He paused. 'Having given Padmavati's hand in marriage to the Rawal, I had planned to request Hammira Chauhan to lead the coalition so as to induce him to join us.'

Not for the first time, Sthaladeva was filled with respect and admiration for his uncle. There were very few kings in their land who would put aside their ego for the greater good. And yet, despite his best efforts and formidable skills in diplomacy, things had gone wrong, just as Sthaladeva had foreseen.

Maharaj Kanhadadeva looked at him wearily, his earlier exuberance all but gone. 'Hammira took offence because I had not seen fit to offer Padmavati to him. To be honest, I thought about it, but despite his many good qualities, Hammira has a cruel streak in him, whereas the Rawal is a kind and gentle man, more suited to our Padmavati. Angered by my decision, he has coldly declined my offer to take charge of the noble endeavour I had envisioned. The good news is that Rawal Ratan Singh was most accommodating and has offered to bring in more people to join our cause.'

Mahisamara shuddered at the thought of his beloved daughter in Maharaj Hammira's harem. Leelavati would not have stood for it and insisted that Sthaladeva revolt against their uncle. He was deeply grateful to Maharaj Kanhadadeva for doing the right thing. 'Hammira Chauhan has proved himself unworthy and is not fit to wipe the ground you walk on, Sire! We are better off without him. The other clans will rally to our cause and the best of us will face the invader together if he chooses to attack us.' Coming from Mahisamara, these were strong words and the king beamed at him.

Sthaladeva said nothing. He was too busy cursing Hammira Chauhan for being so petty and obstinate. Unifying the clans was always going to be an uphill task, now it was an impossibility; too many would throw in their lot with the charismatic Hammira and they would remain as divided as they had always been. Damn the man! And damn the others like him who would always be the downfall of this great land!

8

The New Shah's Vision

If Alauddin Khalji had a weakness, it was for his daily maalish – the powerful massage vigorously rendered by his personal masseuse who accompanied him everywhere. The man used aromatic oils and expert hands to ease the sore, tired muscles of his neck, shoulders, back and limbs, relieving the aches and pains nestled deep in his weary body.

As he skilfully applied circular strokes alternating between his palms, thumbs and elbows, Alauddin groaned in relief. This was when he'd get most of his thinking done. With his body throbbing with pleasure, his mind used the respite to process the endless stream of information fed to him, sifting through the details and formulating winning strategies to make his vision for the future a reality.

Being a powerful shah, he did not lack friends – trustworthy and otherwise – but he always felt that it was his enemies who brought out the best in him. The Mongols were a good example. They stood poised to bring war to his realm and tear apart everything he had built so painstakingly. Famed for their ferocity, fighting skills and formidable endurance, they were worthy adversaries.

His spies had reported that they had brought mighty empires in the distant west to their knees. That when they ran out of food, they cast lots to decide which one of them ought to be consumed to sustain the rest. That they polished their armour using the body fat of their victims who were cooked down to acquire the same. Yet, the danger they posed filled him not with apprehension but a soaring exultation, and he welcomed their advance as he visualized the towering heights of glory he would scale when he smashed them in battle.

His masseuse was now using a wrap made from herbs, spices and clay to firm his body, cleanse him of toxins and rejuvenate him. Alauddin's sense of well-being deepened as his thoughts turned to enemies closer to home that needed to be subdued. Thanks to his informers, he knew all about the ill-fated Rajput coalition that was supposed to have stopped him in his tracks. It was almost funny how these Rajputs sabotaged their own plans, making it easy for him to pick them off one by one.

Rai Karan Vaghela of Gujarat had refused to join the faction headed by Maharaj Kanhadadeva of Jalore, declining to throw in his lot with Hammira Chauhan as well. Karan's prosperous kingdom would make a lovely addition to Alauddin's own burgeoning empire, he decided. It was AD 1299 and before the year was out, Gujarat would be his. Pleasant anticipation flooded his being. He would then turn his attention to Hammira Chauhan of Ranthambore, crush him and help himself to the deposed monarch's land, treasures and women. Chittor ruled by Rawal Ratan Singh would follow. As would Jalore and Siwana.

According to the intelligence reports he had studied, the Rawal was absolutely besotted with his lovely new bride who had been the root cause behind the failed attempt to unify the Rajputs. Given that his wife refused to let him escape her passionate embraces and loving caresses, he was being most derelict in his duty and Chittor was ripe for the picking.

Women! They would be the death of them all. When he captured Chittor and razed it to the ground, would the Rawal think his unreasonable love for this beauty had been worth it? Especially when he executed him and appropriated his wife to adorn his harem?

The shah smiled to himself. The extravagant claims of her extraordinary looks were most likely exaggerated and she simply wouldn't be worth the trouble. Women seldom were.

Once the wrap was removed, Alauddin was led to the hammam where his manservants had ensured that all was in readiness. The shah settled down comfortably on the wooden bench for his steam, which was generated by pouring scalding hot water infused with medicinal herbs on heated stones and released into the closed space through slats made for the purpose.

As he breathed in the vapours and sweated out the accumulated dirt and toxins through his pores, Alauddin turned his thoughts to Maharaj Kanhadadeva's Jalore and to Siwana. It was well known that the valiant old king nursed an abiding hatred for those of the Islamic faith and the shah felt his hackles rise in fury. It was as good a reason as any to crush the man.

He lay face down on his bench as the attendants used loofahs made of coarse hemp to scrub him down, washing his hair and beard with fragrant diluted rose essence. They emptied buckets of water that was piping hot and when his skin felt red hot to the touch, they poured jugs of icy cold water over him. The sudden shift in temperature reverberated through his system, leaving his senses tingling. Then they dried him with towels made with the finest fleece, which felt like the tender caress of a houri.

By his reckoning, the Rajput resistance to his rule would be wiped out in its entirety within the decade. Those who opposed him would be sorry when he beat them, emptied their treasuries and burned their fortresses to the ground with their loved ones inside screaming for mercy. Once he had dealt with the Mongols and Rajputs, he would turn his attention to the Deccan and the rich lands in the south.

When Alauddin emerged fully dressed from his healing session, he was relaxed and glowing. Bursting with good health and utterly rejuvenated, he felt ready for anything. His thoughts turned fleetingly to the famed beauty of Chittor, before his face hardened with dread purpose. It was time to go to war.

9

Chittor

Ratan had been convinced by his in-laws to take a detour to Siwana and spend a few days with them before embarking for Chittor. But they enjoyed themselves so much that the brief visit turned into a month, much to the horror of the queen mother who had not liked the idea of the newly-weds going to Siwana in the first place and had left Jalore in a huff with most of the wedding party.

So when Padma was finally brought to Chittor, people were bursting with expectation. They couldn't wait to see their new queen who was famed as an incomparable beauty. Stories ran wild through the dusty streets – that even stone statues turned their heads so they could drink in Padma's splendour. It was said her skin was so translucent that when she had a sip of sherbet, you could see it go down her throat.

In Siwana, Ratan had told Padma a lot about his beloved land and Leelavati had schooled her so thoroughly on the history of the place, she felt she knew more about Chittor than most people who had lived there all their lives. Much like at her wedding, Padma was overwhelmed when she first beheld the might and grandeur of Chittor. Surya, the Sun God, to whose lineage the Rawals belonged, looked upon this place with great favour. The light was so dazzling and bright it hurt her eyes, and she was grateful for the protection afforded by the odhani covering her face.

Chittor was her home now. And it was beautiful. She was determined to love even the formidable watchtowers and ramparts. On their way in, Ratan pointed out the city's most attractive features but they were mostly lost on her. There were so many pols, shrines and towers that she doubted she would ever be able to get their names right the first time. When Padma saw the Uvar Devi shrine, her breath caught in her throat. It was the most awe-inspiring structure she had seen. Later, she would visit it as often as she could to pray, of course, but mostly to soak in the intense spiritual vibrations of the place and partake of the piping hot prasad.

The numerous parks and gardens with their marble fountains made the place look very picturesque indeed. Padma was particularly taken with the magnificent lakes that dotted the place, which Ratan told her were fed entirely by natural springs. The Haath Kund, where the elephants were bathed, was to become another of Padma's favourites and she would visit it often with her handmaids, armed with bananas and coconuts to feed the gentle giants.

The crowds who had come dressed in their finery thronged the pathways to welcome their king and his new bride. As the sea of bobbing heads gave way for the approaching royal party, their cheers rang out to the heavens.

For the briefest moment, Padma's resolve faltered and she wanted to turn back and run all the way to Siwana. Or lose herself in those forests which dotted the sides of the hill fortress, even if it meant being eaten by lions, tigers or bears. Ratan had not taken Padma's hand in his but his fingers brushed against hers at that precise moment, and she felt better immediately.

~

Before they were taken to the palace, Padma and her groom were led to the Eklinga temple where they prayed and sought the blessings of Ratan's family deity. Only then did they proceed to the palace.

Ratan's mother, the formidable Dhruva Rani, waited

with her aarti thali. At her side was Nagmati, Ratan's first wife, her eyes red and brimming with fresh tears. Despite her grief, Nagmati had chosen to be present, determined to prove she was nothing if not dutiful and to welcome the new sister she had never wanted, even if the effort killed her.

The crown prince, Veer, a gangly adolescent, stood beside his mother, looking sullen. Already, the boys at the gurukul couldn't stop talking about his father's bride in rapturous tones, fuelling many a fantasy and wet dream. Veer was determined to dislike Padma for his mother's sake. Padma winked at him while 'adjusting' her aanchal. The gesture had earned her a spontaneous smile from him and an outraged glare from his mother.

While the queen mother was waving the thali over Padma's head, a piece of burning camphor flew through the air, landing on the hem of the new bride's billowing skirt. Ratan stamped out the sparks with the curved end of his mojari.

The queen mother frowned. 'This is what happens when sons ignore their mothers and go traipsing off instead of returning home after their nuptials!' She glared at her new daughter-in-law. Her manner seemed to indicate that Padma was entirely at fault.

'On the contrary, Mother,' Ratan said firmly, 'Agni, the Fire God, overstepped the line of propriety because he wanted to get closer to my beautiful bride. And who can blame him? I am glad he restrained himself and nothing untoward happened on such a wonderful occasion.'

It would have been a truly wonderful occasion if Agni had given in to his lust and consumed this proud peacock my husband has brought home, reducing her to a pile of ash, thought Nagmati. She visualized her beautiful rival charred beyond recognition and felt much better immediately.

The air was thick with tension as everyone in the gathering stared uneasily at each other. It was Dhruva Rani who took matters in hand.

'What are you waiting for, *Your Highness?*' she barked at Padma. 'Come inside at once and light the lamp before the rest of my hair turns white!'

Padma was so relieved on an impulse she touched the matriarch's feet and the grand old dame was taken by surprise. She hated to admit it but her new daughter-in-law wasn't as hopeless as she had first thought.

Everybody breathed a sigh of relief, glad that a tragedy had been averted. For the moment at least, they were content to ignore the malice that lingered in the air.

10

A Match Made in Heaven

Much later, when they had consummated their love and become the best of friends, if either of them had a regret it was that they could not relive the beautiful moments of their wedding and the memorable night that had followed. They had to content themselves with frequent meanderings through the corridors of memory, lovingly gathering fragments to be replayed and stored carefully. They hoarded every sliver and shard from the past, treating them like precious gems of inestimable value so that they could preserve the magic that had brought them together.

'When I first saw you, I remember thinking it was a good thing you were tall and lean! It would have been a terrifying prospect to resign myself to being mounted by a heavy man built like a mountain, who would have squashed me like a bug!' Padma said, nestling in the crook of his arm. It was late at night but neither of them wanted to sleep.

Ratan gently tugged at a lock of her hair. 'That is what you get for being a liar! You did not think that at all! Besides, even if I had been an obese man, you would have merely said that you had always dreamed of bumping bellies with a paunchy fellow.'

Leelavati had always told her that beauty was the last thing you should look for in a man, but Ratan was something to behold. Padma liked running her fingers through his curly hair or along the length of his shoulders which were hard and firm from the many hours he spent practising archery or his swordplay.

'Let the record show that I have developed a taste for flat, hard bellies! Now tell me, what did you think when you first saw me?'

'Let the record show that you like *a* flat, hard belly and it belongs to *me*.' Padma grinned. Sometimes her husband was a little too possessive of her. 'As to your other question, thankfully, my memory is not a sieve. The bride who had taken refuge behind a gauzy red aanchal that hid her exquisite face took full advantage of that cover and slept through the long-winded ceremony. My buttocks were so sore they would have wept if they could and I lost all feeling in my legs. You, on the other hand, kept your head lowered like the demure bride you were pretending to be and snored through the whole thing. After a point, I was convinced I was marrying Kumbhakarna!'

Padma tugged at his moustache till he yelped. 'Now who is lying?'

'How dare you accuse Rawal Ratan Singh of uttering a falsehood? That is a punishable offence, you know. And as a just man, I will not let you off the hook!' He grabbed a peacock feather from the admittedly ridiculous turban gifted to him by his mother and began tickling her feet with it.

'Stop it or I will scream for the guards! Enough! I'll kill you!' she squealed. 'Everyone claims you are soft on me! If only they knew about the rough treatment I am subjected to at your hands!'

'My legs did fall asleep,' he continued, sticking the feather back into the turban, 'and I stumbled before the saat pheras.'

'You took my hand then . . .' she whispered.

'Yes! I could feel your pulse pounding away as though you were being chased by a pack of wild dogs. I assumed it was the proximity to the handsomest man in the land that was having such a profound impression on the virgin bride!'

'Be serious!' she chided. 'I remember you stroked my

wrist very gently without anyone noticing, till I could breathe normally again. That was the moment I realized that being married to you might not be the worst thing in the world. It is something I'll never forget as long as I live . . .' She slipped her fingers through his.

'It was a beautiful moment!' he concurred. 'And your father had to ruin it by letting loose an explosive fart so malodorous, my nostrils are yet to recover from the unbearable horror!'

Padma threw a cushion at his head. 'You are just jealous because I love my father and he is a wonderful man. And don't get me started on your loving mother. It's not like her farts smell heavenly!'

'Of course not! Only your hair smells heavenly,' he said, burying his face in it. 'Though when you fart, it smells even worse than your father's!'

'Oh! You are such a pig!' Padma wrinkled her nose in disgust. Who would have thought that the king of Chittor would be such a clown and a juvenile one at that? 'I am not going to speak with you if you insist on behaving like a boorish brat who has been spoilt beyond redemption by his mother! Get away from my sight!'

'But we have to discuss the best part – our wedding night!' Ratan cajoled her. 'I was perched on the furthest edge of the bed – shy, terrified and shivering so badly, anybody would have thought I was stricken with fever.

You were gentle, kind, and promised never to hurt me. Then when you had won my trust, you lost no time in ravishing me! And many times I might add!'

'Thankfully, you recovered nicely from the horrors of your wedding night, Your Majesty! It is something no man must be forced to endure . . . You got your revenge though. My favourite ivory bangles were discarded so carelessly I could not find them later! My mother gave them to me and I used to wear them all the time.'

When they began reminiscing about the early days, they could go on and on. Neither remembered the exact moment when they nodded off.

~

Ratan was always up at the crack of dawn. It was the time he set aside to practise his military drills. Padma, on the other hand, allowed herself an extra hour to laze in bed, her husband's heady smell cloaking her in a warm embrace. It made her feel warm, safe, and so very loved. She felt while he was with her nothing on earth could hurt her.

When she returned from her bath, Padma found a new wooden cabinet installed in her chambers.

'What's this?' she asked her giggling maids.

'Open it, Your Highness!' they replied.

She pulled it open and gasped when she saw the contents. For there they were, row upon endless row of ivory bangles, of every conceivable type and pattern.

There were smooth and plain ones, elegant in their simplicity. Some were studded with rare precious stones which included sparkling rubies and gorgeous sapphires. There were a few with delicate gold filigree carvings. Many had engraved images of Goddess Lakshmi, who by some happy accident looked exactly like her. Some had been painted with miniature images of the Rawal and Padma standing next to each other. There were even a few done with delicate brushwork that had captured well-remembered scenes from her beloved Siwana – her dear garden, mango trees, strutting peacocks and her pet rabbits.

Happiness was a delusion, she had always told herself. That she would never ever chase after something so ephemeral and elusive. And yet nothing had prepared her for this. She was happier than she had dared dream possible. In fact, Padma mused as she fingered the bangles, her happiness was complete. She had everything she ever wanted. And always would have as long as her husband was by her side.

There must have been a draught because suddenly Padma's skin prickled with goosebumps. For a brief moment, all she wanted to do was to get between the sheets which smelled of Ratan and drink in his reassuring scent. But she knew that her mother's maids were too efficient and had already remade her bed with fresh silk sheets.

She took a deep breath to steady herself as her maids bustled around, anxious to make sure their mistress looked her best as she set out to face another day of perfect happiness.

11

Love Gone Sour

Raghav Chetana was not a happy man. And his king and queen were not helping his case.

The Rawal and his pretty little wife seemed to derive a perverse pleasure from rubbing his face in their vulgar happiness. Did they really think nobody noticed their 'furtive' glances at each other, full of urgent passion and longing? Not to mention the 'casual' manner in which they allowed their fingers to brush against each other? Or the brazen way in which the Rawal cooed sweet nothings into her ear, not knowing or caring if people were watching? The untrammelled joy they derived from each other was an absolute disgrace, especially since Raghav himself had been most unlucky in love.

He was a short, skinny and unprepossessing man, someone who looked older than his years, but that was probably due to the haughty airs he gave himself for being chosen to serve as one of Rawal Ratan Singh's defence ministers. It was an important position but it did little to enhance his unimpressive personality. He was usually slack-jawed and had a tendency to stare fixedly at random spaces or people. This led people to believe that Raghav was either a drooling imbecile or a creepy pervert.

Fortunately for him, the Rawal tended to look beyond appearances and had recognized his abilities, elevating him to such a respectable position. This stroke of good fortune had given Raghav the confidence to request the hand of his beloved Menaka in marriage. He had been deeply in love with her for the longest time. If her coy glances and bashful ways were any indication, she probably felt the same way, he had convinced himself.

Her fool of a father, who belonged to one of the noblest and most ancient families in Chittor, had failed to take her feelings into consideration and chosen the Rawal's senapati, Dhanpal, for his daughter. The senapati was old enough to be her grandfather. He was so fat and unwieldy, he needed to be helped to his feet after every meeting. He already had a harem full of wives and concubines too. Raghav had quite a sizeable harem himself, though his wives were plain creatures who shut their eyes when he made love to them, lying stiff as corpses beneath him. The trained concubines were worse, with their loud and exaggerated simulation of ecstasy. Only Menaka could make him happy, he knew, but her father had dashed all his hopes.

So what if she was engaged? Raghav would be damned if he allowed his one chance at love to get away from him. He drew up his plan carefully and was going over the details in his mind while strolling along the avenue that abutted the palace, when the Rawal interrupted him.

'You seem to have something on your mind,' he said kindly. 'Whatever it is, it is clearly making you anxious and unhappy. Why don't you tell me all about it?'

Touched by his concern, Raghav was tempted to do so. But then, Rani Padmavati sashayed past them with her gaggle of giggling ladies and the Rawal became distracted as she jangled her bangles at him, making him smile like an adolescent who had just discovered masturbation. By the time his attention returned to his minister, they were joined by others and the moment had passed. Raghav swallowed his fury and irritation and went on thinking about his plans . . .

12

A Palace for the Queen

Trouble followed the lovebirds soon after. It came to a head when Ratan announced his decision to build a palace for Padmavati. She had been happy enough in the harem, but that had been before the attempts on her life.

Her parents, Uncle Sthaladeva and Maharaj Kanhadadeva had been generous and given Padma everything she needed in her married life and enough for the next seven generations. But the most valuable gift had been from her mother, who had provided her with an army of highly trained maids.

Not only did they take care of her every need, they were also fiercely loyal. The entourage was led by the formidable Maitreyi – a handsome woman who had been entrusted with Padma's care and upkeep as a child and whom Leelavati had deemed worthy of taking her place as her daughter's guardian.

Some among her maids were gardeners, and Padma's private garden with its shady pavilions and artistic ponds was the talk of the harem. Quite a few were skilled in the healing arts, and their services which had proved truly efficacious were much sought after. The other ladies wanted to borrow Padma's cosmeticians and hairstylists so they could look like her. Padma never denied anyone anything, much to the annoyance of Maitreyi, who did not understand why these women of means could not buy their own maids.

While Padma had endeared herself to many members of the harem, not everyone was entirely taken with her. It was bound to happen since the Rawal insisted on spending every single night with Padma and had done so without exception since their wedding. The fact that he made it a point to personally ensure the well-being of the other ladies and also find time to enquire about their needs did not change their feelings but rather aggravated them. Since she was in the sunshine of the king's favour, there were those who were jealous but content to stew in their passive dislike for her. Nagmati, the Rawal's first wife, who had decided she loved him only after losing him to Padmavati, was broken-hearted and refused to be comforted no matter how much Ratan tried to pacify her with expensive gifts.

Among the malcontents headed by Nagmati, some were more dangerous than others. A few of the scorned women hired the services of unscrupulous black magicians, who swindled them out of a fortune while promising them that Padma's hair would fall out in tufts, her teeth would blacken and her reproductive parts would shrivel up and die, leaving her barren and causing the king's love for her to sour. When Padma's womb proved infertile despite her apparent sexual shenanigans on a daily basis, they congratulated themselves on the success of their plans.

Things came to a head when a fire broke out in Padma's chambers and the food tasters Maitreyi had hired took ill after sampling the maharani's favourite dishes. Ratan didn't want to take risks with his beloved's safety and decided to provide an alternate accommodation for Padma. Needless to say, this move ruffled a few feathers in powerful places.

~

One morning as they lay in bed, their door burst open and in stomped Dhruva Rani, the folds of her white sari billowing behind her. Usually she summoned Ratan by sending messengers but this time she came unannounced, a shocking departure from her usual style.

Padma got to her feet in a single fluid moment, gathering a discarded chunni in her hand as she rose. If she had been incensed before, now Dhruva Rani was nearly apoplectic with rage when she took note of the fact that her daughter-in-law did not have the decency to look ashamed. Even though her eyes were lowered, Padma stood proud and erect. Ratan, who was hidden beneath the covers, at least had the grace to look chagrined.

'Why can't this creature remain in the harem with the rest of us mere mortals?' Dhruva Rani bellowed, knocking aside a silver platter bearing freshly cut fruit, her bosom heaving with outrage. 'What makes her so special that you feel the need to beggar the kingdom, which is already reeling under the prospect of war, by building a palace for her exclusive use? Has this scrawny minx used the witchcraft passed on by her mother to make you dance to her beat like a monkey in heat? Answer me!'

Why bring my poor mother into this? Padma wondered.

'Such a thing has never been heard of!' Dhruva Rani continued. 'I would rather you were killed than see you become the laughing stock of Chittor. Your enemies will be thrilled to see you bound to a woman who has clearly learned the tricks of the harlot's trade.'

'Mother! Please restrain yourself!' Ratan said in a soothing tone.

Padma wondered how it was possible that the kindest and gentlest man she knew had been born to someone filled with such hate. She knew her husband would rather face the biggest armies in the world single-handedly and unarmed than deal with his mother when she was like this.

'As I already explained to you,' Ratan said firmly, 'I have my reasons for building my wife a palace, even though you may not understand them. But it was you who taught me that a king must act in keeping with the diktats of dharma, and provided he stays true to it, he doesn't owe anybody, not even God, an explanation.'

'You are being ridiculous!' Dhruva Rani huffed. Her stupid son felt the need to protect his new bride, though it was the fool who needed protection from her. 'She spends all her time with the dregs of the kingdom, visiting them in their stinking quarters and whatnot. Imagine that! A royal bride of Mewar consorting with every beggar, cut-throat and whore in the realm just to curry the favour of the great unwashed masses! She has dishonoured you and it shames me that you allow her to do so! It is a good thing your father did not live long enough to see you bring the family name so low. If only the so-called attempts on her life had been successful, this kingdom and I would have thanked every god in the pantheon on our knees.'

Ordinarily, Dhruva Rani's scornful words and contempt would have reduced a lesser woman to a cringing, quivering mess of shame and tears, but Padma was calm and unruffled. When the queen mother stormed off, Ratan took Padma in his arms, soothed her and told her that his mother hadn't always been this way. 'You should have seen her when she was young and happy! Father once remarked he would give up his kingdom just to be at the receiving end of one of her smiles!'

'So what happened? Did your father abandon her for somebody else?' Padma asked curiously.

Her husband nodded. 'Father married many times but till the very end, she held a special place in his heart. It was widowhood that compounded her bitterness. She once complained to me that the only creature lower than a eunuch in the pecking order is a widow, and it was unfair she be made to relinquish the respect which she had earned.'

Padma instinctively knew her husband was suffering because of what had just transpired. Dhruva Rani's words, though directed at her, had wounded Ratan deeply.

'You shouldn't let your mother's words affect you this badly,' she said consolingly. 'It is not unnatural for a lioness to become vicious when it comes to safeguarding the interests of her only child.'

'I try to understand her position and not a day goes by without me paying her a visit . . .' he mused aloud. 'Why then does she say such awful things? If only she attacked me instead.'

'I am not going to die just because your mother wished it!' Padma assured him, but he flinched, so she tried another tack. 'Her back is probably bothering her again. One of my maids is so skilled at therapeutic massages she can fix even the most stubborn ailments. I will send her to the queen mother this very night. We will never be best friends but eventually we will learn to be polite and cordial to each other, I promise!'

'That will be the day!' Ratan smiled in that mischievous way which made him look like a schoolboy. 'But I do hope you are right. How is it that you bear her no ill will, even when you are always at the receiving end of her abuse?'

'As far as I am concerned, your mother gave birth to the most wonderful man in the world and for that alone I will be forever grateful.'

'I too am grateful for you and perfectly willing to forgive you for destroying the formerly beautiful relationship between a mother and her son!' Ratan ducked as she hurled a grape at him. Soon they were laughing so hard as they pelted each other with fruit, they forgot to be upset.

~

Not surprisingly, it wasn't only Dhruva Rani who was vehemently opposed to the new palace. The king's ministers were convinced that their Rawal was too besotted with his pretty wife for his own good and whenever he was in the vicinity, they slyly referred to a certain famous emperor who had come to a bad end because of the passionate love he bore his wife.

'Remember Prithviraj Chauhan?' they whispered. 'He was the greatest of emperors and a warrior without equal. Remember how he destroyed Muhammad of Ghur's armies not once but seventeen times and sent the fanatic back with his tail between his legs?'

'Then he fell in love with his hated adversary Jaichand's daughter, Samyukta, and lost his best men and the cream of the army when he carried her away from the swayamvara,' they murmured in dolorous tones. 'If that were not bad enough, the Rajput coalition he had put together was shattered and Jaichand sent emissaries promising his support to the destroyer from Ghur!'

'Not that Prithviraj cared about the danger he had placed his empire in! He was so enamoured by Samyukta that he forgot his duty to his people and cared only about canoodling with her constantly.'

'He also spent lavishly on Samyukta when he should have been hard at work training his troops, buying weapons, gathering intelligence and working on strategy to drive the invader back.'

'Prithviraj Chauhan could have easily defeated the invader again but Samyukta came between him and the Goddess of Victory, who abandoned him in a huff. Not long after, he was vanquished in Tarain, blinded and left to die. What an ignominious end for the greatest of kings!' They shook their heads sadly.

Even though he was sick to death of these taunts, Ratan went ahead with his plans, defying most of the council and his mother. His mind had already been made up and nothing was going to change it now.

~

Shortly after that, work was begun on the new palace. The Rawal's detractors sniffed in disapproval every time they walked past it. News had reached them that Alauddin Khalji had already begun to act on his grandiose plan to bring not just Aryavarta but the entire world under his dominion. His dreaded legions led by the four notorious Khans had already made incursions into the Deccan and Rajputana. It had been reported that the shah had his sights set on Gujarat. Meanwhile, their Rawal was frittering away precious resources and diverting manpower to build a luxurious abode for his pretty bride! It was most imprudent of him.

'At least Prithviraj proved his worth on the battlefield many times over before he let his foolish fancy for a pretty face turn his brains to mush!' they muttered angrily. The Rawal wasn't deterred and work proceeded at a brisk pace, since he had insisted on making his pet project the top priority. Thanks to his efforts, the palace was ready for habitation in record time.

Rani Padmavati's new home was an architectural marvel, a little slice of heaven itself. It had been cleverly constructed with cut stone around a small lake. It had gardens, an elegant pavilion, graceful arches and pillars inscribed with intricate designs.

The Rawal was inordinately proud of it. He rewarded the chief architect and his team generously, grateful to them for creating a fitting abode for the queen of his heart.

Padma had begged him not to make trouble for himself, insisting that she was perfectly comfortable in the harem, but that was before she had been taken to her new home. Away from the baleful influences of her husband's other wives, she felt free and peaceful. Perhaps her husband's gift to her had been worth all the trouble after all!

For the rest of her days there, every morning Padma would climb to the high terrace of her palace, which afforded a magnificent view of the lake, to drink in the sights and smells of Chittor – a place she had grown to love. She would hold up her face to receive the rays and blessings of the Sun God, thanking him for the abundance he had showered upon her.

13

Justice

'How could you do something so unspeakably evil? That poor girl did nothing to deserve such a terrible fate!'

The Rawal never raised his voice, but he seemed dangerously close to losing his temper, Raghav Chetana noted through the relentless raging of his own personal agony.

Of course, he had not meant for any of it to happen. All he had wanted to do was rescue Menaka from the clutches of the dirty old man she was betrothed to and give her a lifetime of love and happiness. How he had planned to pamper and dote on her!

'The artist has confessed to everything and every single sordid detail has spilled out,' the Rawal was saying. 'You commissioned him to create paintings of that blameless girl in the nude and in the company of a lover, deliberately portraying her in compromising positions! The man actually hid in the baths to make sure he got the intimate details of his subject right. And if that itself weren't unspeakably evil, you had them delivered to the senapati, who promptly called off the wedding but not before giving her family an earful, damaging their reputation by unfairly accusing the girl of lewd and lascivious conduct!'

The Rawal was waiting for him to explain himself, but what could Chetana say? That he had been desperate? That at the time he gave the order for the pictures, he had assumed that once the wedding was called off, her father, anxious to avoid a scandal, would be willing to hand his daughter over to the first suitor who was willing? That he hadn't known the painter had spied on his beloved Menaka? That he couldn't possibly have known that her proud and prickly father would throttle her to death to save their honour?

A strangled sob escaped his lips and he tried to throw himself at his king's feet past the iron bars that separated them, but Ratan Singh stepped back in disgust and Chetana found himself clinging to the unforgiving metal and blubbering incoherently, begging to be spared. He couldn't live without Menaka but he did not want to die either. However, there was no softening the granite countenance of the Rawal, who skewered him with a look of supreme contempt.

'Menaka was innocent and I am going to make sure that she gets justice, even as we speak the crows are feasting on the remains of that odious painter and I dare say they will gorge themselves fit to bursting by the time I am done . . .' the Rawal said with quiet resolve, before spinning on his heels and walking away from his disgraced minister's pitiful entreaties.

What an unholy mess this was! Ratan had to restrain himself from going back and beating the living daylights out of the man who cowered behind the bars, whimpering like the coward he was. They were all going to pay, he swore to himself. He had already forced the senapati to vacate his exalted position and replaced him immediately. This had led to an uproar. The old lion had an army of supporters in court and they were vociferous in protesting their king's decision, which they felt was entirely unwarranted since the so-called victim had clearly been a loose woman with dubious morals and had been carrying on with every male member in her father's household.

Listening to the character slurs, Ratan was tempted to execute the lot of them. Despite repeated calls for reinstating the senapati, he refused to budge. Ratan's anger was aggravated by the fact that the man's birth, position and privilege spared him the full might of the king's justice, which he richly deserved for so callously destroying a girl's life on the most spurious of evidence.

As for her father, Ratan had ruled over the protestations that the man had been well within his rights to act in keeping within the dictates of honour and had sentenced him to death, which created an even bigger furore as his family members trooped in with their supporters wailing and beating their chests, insisting that the patriarch be spared. Even his council members and the queen mother had taken the murderer's side.

'That little chippy you have gone and married has clearly impeded your judgement!' Dhruva Rani lashed out at him.

Ratan thought it was unfair of her to drag Padma into this.

'You will alienate too many powerful people in Chittor,' she continued, 'if you persist in this foolhardy prosecution of the senapati and the idiot who killed his own daughter. It would have been different if you had ruled with an iron fist as befitting a king but you have always been too soft and insisted on listening to the opinions of the fools around you. And now they will bite the hand that feeds them for going against their wishes!'

'What happened to that poor girl cannot go unpunished, Mother!' he insisted quietly.

Dhruva Rani shook her head. 'It was unfortunate but she was born a woman wretched enough to catch the roving eye of an unscrupulous man. When cursed to such a fate, there is nothing anybody can do. If you insist on being so naively idealistic, you will have rebellion in the ranks and that is not something you can risk just because that dead creature was so unlucky!'

She had flounced out of the room when her words fell on deaf ears, but secretly she was glad her son dared not touch the former senapati and risk having the army turn on him. Even the Rawal's lofty principles were tempered with the harsh demands of reality and practical considerations. It had made him furious and he had vented his frustration by executing the painter and would go after the girl's father and Raghav Chetana next. It was such a waste of valuable personnel, according to her. If only she had whipped his stubborn backside bloody when he had been a boy! But his father had insisted on spoiling him and he had grown up to be the Rawal who made bad decisions. The unpleasant Nagmati and the simpering Padmavati were examples of the same.

Ratan was thinking of Padma too and he shuddered inwardly. The world was a cruel place for women and he promised himself that he would die before letting any harm befall her. He would do everything possible to make Chittor a safer place. He was determined to make an example of the offenders in poor Menaka's case. Her father would go to the executioner's block even if his family incited rioting on the streets. Once the deed was done, he would make sure that Raghav Chetana was hanged for his foul deeds and the lot of them could keep each other company in the realm of the damned.

14

Gujarat Is Taken

It wasn't just the fall of Gujarat but the ease with which Alauddin Khalji earned his victory that sent shock waves rippling across Rajputana. Chittor was in a state of high alert and to Ratan's disgust, nearly everybody, including the wisest of his ministers, was convinced that the shah was hiding in the woods and would pounce while they were asleep. Full-blown panic was hardly conducive to formulating decent strategy, Ratan mused as the interminable meetings called to discuss their options turned into shouting matches, with his unruly ministers screaming themselves hoarse as they went over a gamut of suggestions that mostly vacillated between the idiotic and the moronic.

None of them were amenable to the Rawal's suggestion that they join hands with their allies and march against the shah. Ratan knew that Sthaladeva would have agreed with him, but the accursed jyotishis insisted that such an enterprise was frowned upon by the gods and doomed to failure and that he must wait till a more auspicious date could be found. However, in the meantime, there were certain expensive pujas as well as arcane rites and rituals that could be performed which could stop the invader in his tracks, they informed him with infuriating conviction. The Rawal had dissolved the meeting at that point because he was afraid he would give in to temptation and execute the lot of them.

Arriving late from the council meeting which had been even more annoying and ineffectual than usual, Ratan found Padma awake, waiting for him. Usually, she went to bed early. He could sense her anxiety and went to sit beside her.

'What is it that bothers you, my darling?' he said, tucking a stray lock behind her ear.

'You are so preoccupied with the shah that I am starting to think you are obsessed with him and not me, as everybody has assumed. All you do is pore over intelligence reports and consult with your army officers.'

'You are misinformed, my queen,' he whispered into her ear. 'When I am not making a perfect ass of myself with you, I am diverting the resources that ought to be spent on strengthening our fortifications towards building

outrageously expensive monuments in honour of our love.'
There was the faintest trace of bitterness in his voice.

'The problem is you are too tolerant when it comes to
dissent and endless naysaying,' she said. 'You have devoted
your very being to this land and are doing everything in
your power to protect your people. It is high time they
started trusting your judgement.'

'Alauddin is a formidable adversary. The man is
relentless and is surrounded by ruthless people who have
the exact same killer instincts he does.' Ratan paused and
his wife felt the cold finger of anxiety in her heart. He
did not say the words aloud but articulated to himself:
*Men like me have inherited power and we have long taken
our privilege for granted. The shah killed for it and he will
never ever let it go. There is the possibility that despite our
best efforts, the shah will prevail and Chittor will fall.*

The reports were clear. Alauddin was a ruthless leader
and a force to be reckoned with. And his trusted generals,
the four Khans – Ulugh, Zafar, Nusrat and Alap – carried
out his commands with chilling efficiency. There was solid
evidence of their merciless brutality. Even though the
stories of their vices were well known – women, wine,
sodomy and gluttony – they had proved themselves in
battle time and again.

'Tell me more about the shah. I am sick and tired of

idle gossip, but it would be nice to hear your thoughts about this man! Tell me about the fall of Gujarat ...'

'You simply cannot resist knowing everything, can you?' he teased. 'Tell me what you know and I'll fill in the gaps.'

'I'll have you know I merely take an active interest in gathering useful information,' Padma clarified. 'Regarding the conquests of the shah, he took Gujarat with embarrassing ease. Rai Karan Vaghela, the ruler of Gujarat, was caught with his dhoti untied, literally and metaphorically. Ulugh Khan and Nusrat Khan made mincemeat of his paltry resistance and Rai Karan had no choice but to flee. They say his people were not too unhappy to see his back and rejoiced at being delivered from his tyrannical rule. However, when the looting, burning and raping began there was nothing to cheer about. Still, some suggest that order was restored quickly and the miscreants were caught and severely punished. How am I doing so far?'

'That was most succinct, my dear.' Ratan sat up and leaned against the cushions, running his fingers through Padma's glorious mane. 'The Rai's people were disgusted because he escaped with his young daughter, Deval, leaving the populace to be slaughtered by the enemy hordes. So great was his desire to save his own skin, that he left his wife, Kamala Devi, behind. Currently, he is looking for sanctuary with a potential ally to begin the arduous process of recapturing their capital city, Anhilwara Patan, as well as Khambayat and the rest of Gujarat.'

'Is it true that Kamala Devi refused to go with him and spat at his feet?' Padma queried.

'So your spies have told you all about the Rai's sexual peccadilloes, have they?'

'I hear he is the biggest pervert alive, and that he indulged his basest desires in their extreme forms and needed increasingly sadistic thrills to arouse his senses, which had dulled from being saturated in sensuous pleasures. They say his bed slaves have been found broken, bleeding and even strangulated. But soon even this kind of cruelty started to pall and he began to take his pleasures with chaste married women who had the misfortune of catching his roving eye. His pimps would round up these women to be held captive and used mercilessly.' Padma paused to sigh. 'Imagine a king turning on his own people!'

'It is the worst thing to happen,' Ratan added.

'Finally, the Rai's prime minister and two of his generals, whose wives had been abducted and used in this manner, decided they could no longer serve a monster and escaped to Delhi to offer their services to the shah – the Rai's hated adversary.'

'You are right. But we will never know how much truth there is to all this, since most of these outrageous details cannot be verified. One cannot believe gossip and condemn a man!' Ratan said reprovingly. 'But we can safely say the Rai was a deeply flawed human being and an exceptionally awful king. History is most likely to remember him that way at any rate. Before you came into my life, there was a rumour doing the rounds that I welcomed only angelic, curly-haired ten-year-old girls to my bed. Thankfully, you have made a respectable man of me and now they merely think of me as a mad fool in love!'

'Ah! I am so glad I succeeded in taming a reprehensible reprobate! But tell me, what happened to Kamala Devi?'

'You will be pleased to hear that the Khans, acting on the shah's orders, treated her with utmost respect. She was escorted to Delhi under heavy guard where she was taken directly to the harem and provided with every comfort as befitting her status. Now she is married to Alauddin and according to the reports, it was not under duress either.'

'Oh! I love happy endings.' Padmini clapped her hands. Noticing that Ratan looked surprised, she clarified, 'It's not a secret that the shah had a very unhappy marriage with Jalaluddin's daughter. As for Kamala Devi, I hear that a lot of her husband's victims were dear friends of hers and that the Rai tied her up and made her watch because her distress and tears enhanced his own pleasure.

Perhaps she will persuade the shah to devote his life to love and not war?'

'Only you are capable of seeing Alauddin Khalji as a romantic.' Ratan smiled. 'Public opinion is very much against them. The shah stands accused of coveting and capturing another man's wife. As for poor Kamala Devi, the people think she ought to have killed herself rather than surrender her virtue to the enemy. As far as I am concerned, the queen of Gujarat is a remarkable woman and deserves better than the likes of Rai Karan or Alauddin Khalji.'

'It was brave of her to choose to live rather than throw her life away over the likes of that repulsive Rai,' said Padma. 'At least the shah knows how to treat a lady like her with love and affection.'

'I am not sure love and affection come into Alauddin's calculations. Muslims are legally allowed to take four wives, and since Kamala Devi is renowned for her beauty and worshipped by her people, he was probably advised to marry her. Also, it was a move guaranteed to crush the spirit of the people of Gujarat.'

When Ratan saw that Padma looked crestfallen by his assessment, he hastened to pass on tidings that would be more to her liking. 'Since you love happy endings so much, you will be pleased to know there is evidence that the shah has shown her favour and been most kind. Kamala

Devi was anxious about her poor daughter who was in the clutches of her husband. When she shared her fears with Alauddin, he sent one of his Khans to impress strongly upon King Ramchandra of Devagiri, where the Rai had taken refuge, that he would be better off being loyal to the throne of Delhi and find and restore Deval to her mother. The mission was successful on both counts. The princess of Gujarat is currently engaged to Alauddin's son, Khizr Khan.'

Padma's smile lit up the entire room and Ratan's heart lifted at the sight. 'Perhaps he will be content with the rich booty he captured from Gujarat . . .' she began hopefully.

'I am afraid that is wishful thinking, my dear.' Ratan shook his head sadly. 'He is one of those men whose sole purpose in life seems to be war. The shah believes he is destined to be the emperor of the largest realm in the history of the known world. He refers to himself as Sikander Sani, after the Macedonian conqueror who came all the way to our land and defeated King Paurava. Unlike that fellow, Alauddin has no plans of turning back. The question now is not whether he will attack but when and where he will choose to strike. It could be at the heart of Mewar, or Ranthambore, Jalore, Malwa, perhaps even the Deccan.'

'Let him do his worst!' Padma said staunchly. 'He can call himself whatever he wants but he will never be able to match you in strength and valour. Besides, if there is justice in the world, the criminal who stole a throne by murdering his own king and kin will never triumph over a righteous man.'

Ratan hoped the fates were listening. In his knowledge, they tended to favour the mighty over the noble. He supposed there was nothing to do but make his preparations carefully and do everything in his power to save Mewar from whatever force came its way.

Padma drew Ratan to her chest and held him close till he fell asleep. As she tucked him in like a mother would a child, she admired his handsome features which were so resplendent even in repose.

'You are the better man,' she whispered to him, 'and you will triumph. You must! For Chittor and us!' Gently she kissed his forehead.

Ratan smiled in his sleep. That night he dreamed of victory.

15

Out of the Frying Pan

Raghav Chetana was having a sleepless night. It was hardly surprising, since he was supposed to be hanged tomorrow. Ironically, he was willing to give his very life to escape his fate. Despite strong opposition, the Rawal had remained adamant and Menaka's fool of a father had been executed. Now, it was his turn and nobody seemed inclined to intervene on his behalf.

He had been wallowing in misery and self-pity ever since, when he was not crying and bemoaning his fate for all the world to hear. The guards had promised to knock his teeth out if he did not hush up. They had done just that when he made the foolish decision to call out to the gods to save him.

The disgraced minister started when a heavily robed apparition emerged from the shadows and began undoing his restraints. Raghav wondered if he had finally succumbed to the madness that had threatened to engulf him. When he was free, he got to his feet shakily and dressed hurriedly in the clothes that were held out to him. Wordlessly, his benefactor led him out of the dungeons, following a twisting path that despite his condition he took care to memorize.

Once they were clear of the fort, his rescuer addressed him, and to his surprise it was in a dulcet, unmistakably feminine tone. 'The goddess who has rescued you from the jaws of death demands nothing but unswerving fealty and your willingness to carry out her every wish.'

'I am a willing slave of the merciful goddess!' Raghav intoned reverentially, even though he had a premonition that he was getting into something dangerous. He knew this was nasty business, and that he would do well to return to his prison cell and the hangman's noose that awaited him. But the prospect of freedom and a future that did not involve him hanging by the neck till he died proved to be an irresistible lure.

The creature in front of him seemed pleased and as she drew closer to him, her musky scent made his pulse quicken. She bent forward and whispered into his ear. When Chetana heard the command in his ear and realized the full implication of it, he stiffened with horror.

Goddess indeed!

He would throw himself off the highest watchtower in Chittor before acceding to the wishes of this she-devil!

Once again the fiend whispered in his ear, laughing throatily as she said, 'None of your fine scruples now, you devious bastard. Do as you are told and earn riches beyond your wildest longing. If you fail, we will hack off every one of your limbs, leaving you to beg on the streets while your mother, sisters and daughters will be sold off into brothels where their customers will take what remains of your family's honour.'

She waved cheerily as Raghav left by stealth with the horse and provisions that had been arranged for him. He wept all along the way, but the abomination that had rescued him from certain death only to damn him to something far worse, was unmoved.

~

Ratan was in the foulest of moods once the disappearance of Raghav Chetana was discovered. How could his guards have failed him so badly? How could *he* have failed Menaka so badly? Though his men had scoured the countryside, they could find no trace of Chetana. Ratan ordered the guards who had been left in charge of the prisoner to be severely punished. Not that it made him feel any better.

Raghav had to have had help and it was clear that his enemies within Chittor had been working overtime to make this happen. He could not shake off the feeling that he was missing a crucial piece of the puzzle.

Padma, who had been following the case most avidly, had a philosophical slant on the matter. 'He will get his comeuppance,' she said staunchly. 'You defied so many to make sure that poor Menaka's tragic demise did not go unpunished. Some things are always beyond human agency. The gods probably felt that death was too good for the likes of Raghav Chetana; they must have intervened to make sure his punishment is all the more excruciating.'

Ratan knew that was supposed to be comforting but wondered why he did not feel any better. He had a feeling that this nasty business was far from over.

'Is it true that when the painter's working quarters were searched they found pictures of many more high-born ladies engaged in taboo acts?' she queried.

Ratan did not reply but his thoughts went back to the filthy things they had discovered among the painter's possessions. He had personally ensured that every last one of them had been consigned to the flames where they belonged. Just thinking about it made him want to kill the man all over again.

16

The Traitor

Alauddin Khalji simply could not stand the sight of traitors. And the cowering wretch before him was the very embodiment of one. The man was perspiring profusely, reeking of powerful bodily odours, though he had been allowed to bathe and dress in fresh clothes before being ushered into the shah's presence at his hunting lodge near Jalandhar. Perhaps he should have been doused in perfume as well. He hated how his lips were parted all the time, making him look like a blubbering buffoon. Yet, he knew the value of treacherous vipers who had served his cause admirably in the past.

Most of his ilk were in the business of betrayal for money or because they felt they had been ill-treated by their sovereigns. Some just liked to cast their lot with the one they believed would be the eventual victor. But this

Raghav Chetana was a puzzle. He seemed determined to make trouble for Rawal Ratan Singh, the king of Mewar, who had pissed all over his love story or something equally pathetic. But it was also apparent that he was bitterly conflicted, though he did a passable job of masking it.

Alauddin Khalji listened impatiently to the idiot blather on and on about why he ought to invade Chittor immediately if not sooner, especially since that had been his plan from the very beginning. That was the problem with small-minded morons – they did not dream big. Forget Gujarat, Chittor, Ranthambore and the lands to the south, he wanted to conquer the entire world and see what lay beyond the sun, moon and the stars as well as the very last frontiers known to mankind. All he wanted was everything!

'... her beauty is beyond compare! Why, they say even the gods are enamoured of her beauty. The Rawal is so hopelessly besotted with her and listening to her council stripped the powerful Senapati Dhanpal of his command!'

The traitor whined on and Alauddin tried to mask his exasperation. Whoever sent this puppet clearly had no notion as to the working of his own superior and subtle mind.

Imagine going to war over a woman! Besides, wasn't this the same troublemaker Hammira Chauhan had wished to marry, refusing to join the Rajput coalition because she had been betrothed to Rawal Ratan Singh? His curiosity was piqued. He thought of his late wife, Malika Jahan, and suppressed the urge to laugh. Even the beautiful and relatively docile Kamala Devi, who could be counted among the treasures of his Gujarat campaign, had become something of a bore.

'In Chittor, everyone believes she is a reincarnation of Goddess Lakshmi,' the man was saying, 'and she is the very embodiment of not just beauty but virtue as well. She is so modest, no man has seen her face in its entirety except her husband. The people worship the ground she walks on and insist that the man lucky enough to possess her will be blessed with prosperity and victory in all his endeavours.'

Alauddin was bored. It was bad enough these people worshipped so many gods and goddesses, wasting their time by fighting over which religious sect was the greatest and spilling blood needlessly, now they had clearly started revering unworthy mortals as well. If they had a smidgen of sense, they would prostrate themselves at his feet since their lives and lands would belong to him ultimately. In fact, he would do a far better job of improving their lot in life than their gods and petty squabbling kings. He couldn't do worse at any rate.

As for this Chetana, he was an even bigger fool if he thought a great shah like himself would go traipsing off to war for the sake of a local beauty. Alauddin held up his hand and the fool ceased his incessant prattling about his queen's translucent skin and fine hair.

'When you are summoned before my war council, if you repeat any of this nonsense I will have your tongue wrenched out and fed to the crows while you watch,' Alauddin barked at the coward, who gulped noisily. 'Never forget that Alauddin Khalji does not need the help of a false goddess to prosper and emerge victorious.'

The man nodded furiously as Alauddin continued, 'You will tell my generals that your queen and her besotted husband are fanatical Hindus, who have sworn to drive out those of the true faith back to the hellhole from which they emerged. That they perform evil rituals and black magic to urge their gods to strike my people with disease and misfortune. You will swear that the little queen refers to us as bastards with bald pricks and has made her husband swear to castrate the foreign invaders who are raping both their women and their land. Do you understand?'

It was a magnificent speech that would have his Khans frothing at the mouths, making them a hundred times more belligerent and warlike than they already were. They were capable men but a little added incentive and religious fervour, rather than talk of an exquisite queen, would get them truly worked up.

Raghav Chetana swallowed again and his tongue tripped over itself as he sought to assure the shah that he would assiduously repeat the words he had been taught.

Alauddin watched as the guards dragged Chetana away from his presence, the shah's thoughts buzzing with new ideas.

He leaned back against his sumptuous divan and took in the opulence of his surroundings disinterestedly. The painted panels, spectacular trellis work, Persian carpets and luxurious furnishings did little to lift his spirits. Only the business of war and the promise of glory distracted him from the restlessness that had long robbed him of peace.

Alauddin mulled over what he'd just heard. Chittor's disgraced commander-in-chief presented an array of interesting possibilities. Surely this Senapati Dhanpal would not think twice about accepting a new respectable position, fine palaces, land and women, not to mention more gold than he could possibly spend in the years left to him. Fortunately, there was no dearth of traitors like the sorry specimen who had just been ushered out of his presence, and one could easily be found to make an offer on the shah's behalf to interested parties.

A wicked grin spread across Alauddin's features as he accepted the single goblet of wine he allowed himself every day. What would he do without the traitors he loathed and needed in equal measure? They would no doubt be happy to deliver not just Chittor but Ranthambore and the rest of the Rajput strongholds to him.

He sighed in satisfaction and allowed his thoughts to dwell lazily on the fabled beauty of Chittor, who had inadvertently proved so instrumental to his plans, and his smile deepened. He was already looking forward to verifying for himself if she was as exquisite as they all said.

Alauddin Khalji rose to his feet as he contemplated his next move. Raghav Chetana seemed desperate for him to march to Chittor. Consequently, the shah was determined to spite the traitor and frustrate his plans. He would leave Ratan Singh alone for a little longer and focus his attention on other Rajput kingdoms that needed taming instead. Perhaps he would march against Maharaj Kanhadadeva, who had foolishly refused the hand of friendship that had been offered to him prior to the Gujarat campaign and needed a lesson in manners.

In the meantime, the Mongols with whom his men had fought a pitched battle at Jalandhar a year before he took Gujarat were on the march again. Not that he was worried. It would be easy enough to send them scurrying. And there were reports that a rebellion might be brewing among his own subjects. A lesser man would have been confused about the best plan to make, given the circumstances, but the shah was a predator and had the same infallible instincts. If he waited patiently, he would know exactly when to strike. And where.

17

Calm before the Storm

Padmavati was a child of the great outdoors. Even her opulent palace couldn't induce her to remain within closed doors for long. And since Chittor had such beautiful temples, she couldn't wait to step out every morning. Her new-found spirituality surprised Maitreyi, her chief maid.

'Why this sudden interest in places of worship? When you were a wee mite you kicked up an almighty fuss before every temple visit, saying that the priests with their incantations, rites and rituals were the most tedious creatures in all existence!'

Padma only smiled mischievously. She had become a great one for observing religious strictures and visiting every single temple in Chittor as frequently as possible to pray for the well-being of her husband, the prosperity of the realm, to beseech the gods and goddesses individually to bless her with sons and urge them to ease her mother-in-law's ailing back.

Dhruva Rani was suspicious of these temple visits, but her daughter-in-law looked so sincere, excessively so in her opinion, that she was willing to condone her actions if it meant the possibility of many grandsons in the immediate future and relief from her accursed bodily ailments, which were already much better thanks to the gods and the ministrations of Padma's well-trained masseurs.

So Padma rambled all over the countryside in her devotional fervour, usually making an outing of it, taking along whoever was willing to join her and packing picnic lunches in case they got peckish.

Padma visited the Uvar Devi temple as frequently as possible. She became fast friends with the priests there who she claimed were the least sanctimonious and uptight in all of Chittor. Besides, they were far more amenable when it came to implementing her wishes for the welfare of her people.

'Your mother would disapprove of this lunacy!' Maitreyi complained when her charge outlined the charitable schemes she was determined to carry out.

But Padmavati only laughed.

Wherever she went, the crowds followed. They gathered around her, hoping for a glimpse of their beautiful queen. Women approached her seeking to bless or be blessed, to share their troubles or present their babies to her, asking that she honour the little ones with a name of her choosing. Padma was comfortable with her people and always took the time to listen to what they had to tell her, much to the discomfiture of those who accompanied her on these expeditions.

At her insistence, Maitreyi was told to bring a large bag of copper coins which Padma would distribute among the poor. A bodyguard would carry another bag filled with eatables for the street urchins, who crowded around her demanding stories and sweets.

'They ought to be content with rooting about in the trash where they belong instead of having the temerity to demand treats from their queen,' Maitreyi would mutter. As always, she was ignored even by the grubby mites.

The children would eat their fill of the goodies as Padma sat under a tree – unmindful that her royal garments had never been intended for sitting on dirty grounds – and told them a few stories.

Their favourites were the ones about Chittor, especially a myth about Bhima, the second Pandava brother, who had the strength of a hundred elephants. Bhima had supposedly raised the Chittor fortress overnight at the behest of two yogis – Nirbhayanath and Kukareshwar – who had promised to give him the fabled gemstone, parasmani, which could turn anything it touched into gold, if he performed this impossible feat. Bhima accepted this challenge and took on the task with fervour. When the yogis realized that Bhima would likely complete the task with time to spare, they grew anxious; they didn't want to lose the parasmani. The last day for the task to be completed drew close. Before the dawn of the final day, the yogis began to urge the rooster to begin crowing earlier than it usually did. Thinking he had failed, Bhima stamped his feet in fury, creating the lake they called Bhimtal. After her tale, the children would rush to the spot to gape at its historical significance.

'Must you fill their impressionable minds with nonsense?' Ratan would complain later. 'I wonder who makes up these far-fetched stories and spreads them as irrefutable fact . . . The truth is Chittor was built during the reign of the Mauryas. Bappa Rawal snatched it from their last ruler. This version is less stirring but at least it isn't as ridiculous as the one you have been bandying about!'

Maitreyi shuddered when she took note of the runny noses of the street urchins, their tattered garments, louse-ridden unwashed hair, and begrimed bodies. On returning to the palace, she would scream for the maids to prepare a warm bath and scrub Padma with coir so roughly that her skin would turn pink.

'I have to agree with the queen mother . . .' Maitreyi

would mutter under her breath. 'The rani of Chittor cannot allow the rabble to get close to her royal person. What will your mother say when she hears they touched you with their filthy paws! Disease-carriers, the lot of them. And you with your delicate constitution . . . what will I tell your mother if you were to fall sick? She will have the skin flayed off my back, not that you seem to mind endangering my poor person.'

'Even if you were not under my protection, nobody who cared a mite about their own lives would risk laying a finger on your body!' Padma replied. 'Why, you are so tough! I keep telling Ratan if he were to give you command of the army you would send the Muhammadans howling back to their mothers.'

Maitreyi was so pleased with Padma's words she used a gentler touch while sponging her with cold milk next. She was proud of her baby who had grown up to be such a worthy queen.

The dai applied her special concoction made with over thirty ingredients, which she swore was a sure guarantor of eternal youth and unfading looks, all over Padma's body, ignoring her faint protestations. Padma hated sitting still while the goop hardened. Maitreyi refused to allow her to talk while the mask did its work, insisting that if she so much as moved a facial muscle, her face would become wrinkled as a crone's.

'And the vile stories those accursed creatures fill your ears with!' Maitreyi ranted. 'Miserable bitches who probably deserve the beatings their husbands mete out to them. They tell fanciful tales of life-threatening illnesses, crushing poverty and whatnot just to get you to loosen your purse strings. And you are so gullible you oblige every single time!'

'It doesn't matter whether their stories are true or fabrications,' Padmavati said thoughtfully. 'Nearly all of them can use the money because they have so little. If it makes their lives just a little bit more comfortable, I will not grudge them a few coins. And truth be told, I like being out there,' she added dreamily. 'It feels more real and somehow less oppressive than here. Ratan has purpose in his life, whereas all I am supposed to do is dress myself up like a doll and keep still. Tell me . . . what good has that ever done anyone? I want to feel useful and while there is life in me, I will always strive to make it count.'

Maitreyi did not say the words out loud but Padmavati knew what she was thinking. Her restlessness would vanish as soon as she was with child. Why did people always assume babies were the cure for all the ills in their world? Her dai refused to give up hope but Padma suspected it might never happen. Strangely, despite the happiness her barrenness brought her detractors, it didn't bother her too much. And she had Ratan to thank for that.

~

'There may be a good chance I cannot ever bear you children, though we couldn't possibly try any harder,' Padma said, using a determinedly breezy voice after a particularly painful encounter with her mother-in-law, who had asked the raj vaidya to prescribe a dozen foul-tasting potions to help make her fecund. 'And I am not going to go mad with grief if you decide to plough more fertile fields or whatever it is that men seek to do when they decide to bed a different woman every night of the year. I don't understand that kind of berserk promiscuity in men, especially since the prostitutes who are guilty of the same, despite having far less choice in the matter, are so universally reviled.'

'Haven't you heard? I couldn't cohabit with a different woman every night of the year even if I wanted to because a certain enchantress from Siwana has entrapped me with her black magic and spells,' Ratan accepted the punch she threw at his shoulder manfully before drawing her to his chest. 'In your arms, I have found all the happiness and peace I could wish for and it would be greedy to expect anything more. If we are meant to have children, then we will. If it does not happen, we still have no cause for complaint as long as we have each other.'

'But this is too serious an issue for you to jest about,' Padma scolded. 'Your mother and ministers are constantly complaining about your lack of enthusiasm in ensuring the continuity of your line.'

'In the Mahabharata, Gandhari had a hundred sons but it did not ensure that a single one of them would secure the throne of the Kurus, and it certainly wasn't for lack of trying. I hope that Veer will rule after me and do a far better job, but it is up to the fates to decide if my line will prevail hundreds of years from now. And I don't see any reason to worry about things that do not fall under my purview.'

Padmavati knew he was thinking of the thrice-cursed war that was looming not too far in the distance. No matter how many times she wished and prayed for the war to not happen, it insisted on drawing ever closer.

When she spoke her voice was muffled. 'Since you are the king, you can do as you please. Let's run away from here and never come back. We will find a place, a tiny hovel in the deepest part of a forest, which will serve our needs perfectly. It will be just the two of us. Then we won't have to deal with shahs who want to rule the three worlds, the pressures of ruling a kingdom, the ire of rejected women or any of the endless demands they make on us.'

'I'll miss my mother too much!' Ratan whispered into her hair. 'And you will miss the culinary delights served up by our chefs, and having Maitreyi take care of your needs, including the wiping of your tender backside. Otherwise, I would have agreed to leave this instant.'

Padma tried to laugh but it was more of a whimper. 'You can learn to cook and wipe my tender backside! And I promise I'll take care of you even better than your mother.'

'Tempting though the prospect is, I want you to remember that it is just the two of us even when we are surrounded by my ministers and your maids, with Maitreyi peeking over my shoulder and giving me the evil eye for making you cry like this. It will always be the two of us against the rest of the world.'

'I never cry!' Padma insisted and they lay in each other's arms for a long time, drawing all the comfort they could from each other till they fell asleep.

Her lack of children may not have been driving her to distraction, but it was clearly bothering her detractors a lot more than Alauddin's advances. Even the Rawal's most loyal followers and obsequious sycophants pointed out that it might be better for him as well as the kingdom if he were to divide his time and affections a little more equally among his wives and concubines, especially since some of the others were more capable of bearing him strong sons to secure the succession and beautiful daughters to make beneficial political alliances.

'Too many sons are every bit as bad as no sons.' Ratan would laugh at the well-meaning efforts of his courtiers to prise him away from Padma. 'They would all believe they have an equal right to the throne and tear apart the kingdom with civil war. Veer is the heir apparent and secure in his right. Besides, wouldn't our time be more gainfully employed if we discussed further fortifications of the city, as we had originally set out to do, instead of having this futile discussion about whom I choose to spend my nights with?'

Dhruva Rani had the eunuch who took care of her affairs keep a lookout for the most desirable girls whose mere gaze could make a man wild with excitement. There were dainty yellow-skinned girls from a faraway place with skin softer than rose petals, exotic Arabian dancers whose bellies seemed to have a life of their own and a bevy of beauties from Ceylon, far to the south. They were paraded before the king every single day.

Between his meetings with his commanders and intelligence briefings, Ratan didn't have time to devote to pleasure and so he entrusted these women to Padma's care. His wife lost no time in taking them under her wing. Soon, they were every bit as invested as she was in trying to rescue the city's unfortunates from themselves. 'It is more satisfying than working on my back and knees . . .' one of the slant-eyed women told Maitreyi, and Padma's dai wondered if she would feel the same way when she realized there were no strings of pearls, fine silks and bulging purses of gold coins in this line of work.

Consulting the priests at her beloved Uvar Devi temple and ignoring Maitreyi's impassioned protests, Padmavati donated a large amount of gold to them so they could refurbish some old, decrepit buildings on their property to house the poverty-stricken among the populace. Those afflicted with disease could avail themselves of the services of a decent physician, homeless individuals could rest in comfort and every layabout in the land who hadn't done an honest day's work could expect to get a hot meal.

The inhabitants of Chittor were now convinced that Padmavati was indeed Goddess Lakshmi come to save them all from the clutches of the Muhammadans who were advancing towards them. Many had taken to worshipping her, waiting patiently outside the palace gates for her blessing. Some claimed that they had seen her perform miracles and save the lives of their brats with the merest smile or a light touch.

Ratan thought it was hilarious and related the news to Padma about her induction into Godhead. She was not amused, especially since the Khalji shah was a lot closer than any of them would have liked. The very thought of an almighty clash for Chittor and Mewar filled her with dread. She was most worried when Ratan made an effort to sound cheerful and allay her fears, masking his own simmering tension and umpteen frustrations. Sometimes he was every bit as bad as Maitreyi and insisted on treating her like a child.

When she tried to probe about the shah and his advancement, his answers were vague and unsatisfactory. Or sweet but framed with the purpose of deterring more questions on matters which he clearly cared not to discuss with her.

'When I come in here, it is like being in a different place, an island of beauty and tranquillity . . .' he said. 'I see you sitting with your feet trailing in the water, feeding your swans and fish, allowing the latter to nibble on your toes, humming as you string glass beads together to form intricate patterns. Your idea of a perfect day is when the chefs send you rabadi as a surprise. When I see your carefree spirit and the joy you spread around with so much ease, all I want to do is suspend time and preserve those perfect moments forever. It makes me forget the smell of sweating men hunched over a table, playing at solving the problems they are plagued with, and the safety of the multitudes of men and women in my care whose future is tied to the decisions of their king. When I think of you it makes me smile, even if there is precious little to feel happy about.'

His speech left her feeling helpless. She was happy to do whatever she could for him but he clearly did not want to trouble her. She could, however, feel his terrible loneliness, the crushing burden of his responsibilities, and wished there was something she could do to alleviate it. Mostly she was happy to be his woman but there were times when she wished she were a man who could help shoulder his burden, give him sage advice and ride with him into battle.

18

Men and War

Ratan supposed he had seen it coming.

Senapati Devadutta, who had replaced Dhanpal, brought him the bad news. 'Five of our foremost divisions have revolted and withdrawn to Haldighat. These were the troops who had been ordered to secure our borders when the shah's army was headed for their Gujarat conquest. They discharged their duties faithfully but certain vested interests have caused them to betray their true king.'

'What are their terms?' Ratan asked, pleased to note that his tone was firm even though his heart was broken. These were his men and he had done his best by them, often paying and equipping them from his personal stores. And this was how they had seen fit to repay him. Worst of all, they had abandoned Chittor. If Alauddin marched against them now they would be sitting ducks.

And to think he had been preparing to take the initiative, gather his troops and march against the shah, now that the jyotishis had fixed a suitable date!

'They demand that Senapati Dhanpal be reinstated at once, Sire. His supporters insist he has served the realm faithfully and you have insulted him by stripping him of his rank over the matter of an immoral girl whom the gods saw fit to punish.' To his credit, Devadutta was crisp and concise.

'The only mistake I made was to let him get away with his unforgivable conduct. I should have stripped him of his rank, confiscated his lands and struck off his head with my sword!' Ratan said. 'We will not give in to the demands of the rebels and if they can find it in their hearts to turn their backs on Chittor, they do not deserve to fight to save their homes and families. We are better off without them.'

Neither of them remarked about the fact that the shah's spies would have informed him about the defection of Senapati Dhanpal's loyalists and that Chittor was vulnerable in the event of a direct attack.

Devadutta cleared his throat to express his disagreement before saying, 'Then we must rethink our strategy, Sire. We cannot risk open war and must prepare for a siege.'

'So be it!' Ratan nodded with an equanimity he did not feel. 'Send word to our allies, especially the Chauhans,

Lakshman Singh of Sisodia and the Bhils. Any help they can offer will be appreciated. Summon our military advisers as well as our best builders. Together, we will make Chittor the most impenetrable fortress in the land!'

Devadutta hastened to do his bidding. But Ratan could feel the despair in the man's soul. Especially since it mirrored his own.

~

Padmavati was bursting with impatience to share her news with Ratan. Nowadays he was so busy examining fortifications, consolidating alliances, conferring with his military advisers and the rest of the business of fighting a war, he usually crawled under the sheets with her as dawn was approaching and rose again with the sun. Despite the tremendous pressure he was under, Ratan always maintained his composure and was never irritable or short with anyone.

Maitreyi was trying to get Padma to calm down and eat something but she was too anxious for food.

'Can you believe that my grand-uncle, Maharaj Kanhadadeva, has actually defied the shah? It is too exciting and terrifying for words. I wish Ratan was here so I could tell him this.'

'In all likelihood, he is already aware of the situation.'

The words were uttered in the tone she used when dealing with children and the simple-minded. 'Besides, all this anxiety and stress will heat your blood and make you sick. Why don't you sit down for a moment like a lady instead of pacing about like a caged lion, and I'll repeat everything I have already told you about the news from Siwana and Jalore!'

Padma obliged. Queen or not, Maitreyi would order her about just as she pleased.

'Before the conquest of Gujarat,' Maitreyi began, 'the shah's forces under Ulugh and Nusrat Khan sent Maharaj Kanhadadeva their leading diplomats and the renegade generals of Rai Karan headed by his former prime minister, Madhavan, whose wife had killed herself because the Rai had violated her modesty. They wanted to negotiate passage through Maharaj Kanhadadeva's lands to bring down Karan.'

Padma was agog with interest and bristling with impatience when Maitreyi paused, attempting to feed her a mouthful of goonda ki sabzi as though she were still a toddler, making her splutter angrily, 'You promised to tell me all the news! And I don't want any more green berries!'

'If I know anything at all about Maharaj Kanhadadeva, and I think I do, he would not have been swayed by any arguments or rich presents and robes of honour. He has an abiding hatred of the Muslims and dreams of the day when every last one will be driven from our land. Ratan . . . I mean, the Rawal told me that notions such as these are antiquated because the Muslims have made this land their home for many generations now and they too belong here every bit as much as we do.'

'Yes, this land belongs to Hindus, Muslims, Jains, Buddhists and even those subscribing to the new faiths, but communal harmony is a long way off and humans would need to figure out how to fly across the skies and take a walk on the moon before they learn to love their brethren. For now, we must wage endless wars with each other.'

Maitreyi, in addition to being a stolid reactionary with a sarcastic tongue, was not one to give up and shoved into Padma's mouth a piece of roti dipped in kairi gravy, and the spicy tang of the mangoes made Padma's eyes water. But it was so delicious she did not protest and her dai watched her chew and swallow with great satisfaction. She fed her another mouthful before resuming her narrative.

'As I was saying, Maharaj Kanhadadeva refused to receive the delegation, accusing them of base treachery, and dismissed them as traitors for throwing in their lot with the Muslim invader. He sent the messengers back with a very insulting reply . . .'

When Padma had been little, Maitreyi would lull her

with long, colourful stories and feed her to the point of bursting. She was doing the same now. Padma was too heavily invested in the riveting news to stop her, though she knew that if her dai had her way she would be big as the elephants they fed at Haath Kund soon. Still, she chewed the flaky roti softened with gravy, and listened.

'Maharaj Kanhadadeva refused them passage on the grounds that they were petty scoundrels without honour who would ravage the countryside, ravish their virgins, rob the populace and ransack their homes. He also accused them of being cattle thieves, eaters of sacred bovine flesh and accursed destroyers of the Somnath temple,' Maitreyi said with relish.

'I think it was brave of him to take a stand against the shah,' Padma asserted. 'How dare the shah assume that Maharaj Kanhadadeva would join him in his mass-murdering spree? I would have preferred if my grand-uncle had killed the two Khans and destroyed their army instead of merely provoking them by refusing Chauhan hospitality and insulting them. Unfortunately, as a consequence, thousands of innocent civilians paid the price in full for his hauteur as they cut a bloody swathe across Gujarat. A little diplomacy would have served him better.'

'There is more! Earlier I didn't want to frighten you with the implications of Maharaj Kanhadadeva's defiance.'

Ratan had entered the room. The Rawal's voice was hoarse and his face drawn with fatigue, and he appreciated the chilled drink that was pressed into his hand.

Maitreyi bowed and withdrew with great speed but not before making Padma swallow some honey-infused water.

'Alauddin's generals were in two minds,' he continued. 'They wanted to punish your grand-uncle by laying siege to Jalore. But they were bound by the shah's orders and he had told them to take Gujarat first. However, to teach Maharaj Kanhadadeva a lesson, they took a little detour to Somnath and ransacked the famous temple yet again and stole the idol. They intend to return to Delhi with it and use the pieces to pave the pathway leading up to a mosque.'

Padma undressed him herself, trying to still her pounding heart, wiping him down with a soft cloth soaked in rose water, and kneaded his tired muscles with fragrant oil, massaging and soothing his scalp before feeding him a light meal. She was possessive of their time together and hated for the maids to intrude. She waited patiently for him to finish eating.

'You were telling me about the situation in Jalore. Maharaj Kanhadadeva must have sent for Uncle Sthaladeva and Father . . .' she coaxed, kneading the muscles on his shoulders and back that were knotted with tension. Ratan groaned with relief. 'Since Gujarat has already fallen, is that Ulugh Khan going to besiege Jalore next? My uncle and father must be on their way there!' she prompted him, hoping against hope that somehow such a crisis had been averted.

'Your Uncle Sthaladeva and father have been ordered to hold down Siwana.' Padma breathed easier at once. Ratan shook his head tiredly. 'Jalore was not really in Alauddin's sights and will be safe for the time being at least, though Maharaj Kanhadadeva's precipitous words have ensured a day of reckoning in the future. But spurred by their success in Gujarat, the Khalji army decided to march past Jalore, ignoring Maharaj Kanhadadeva's refusal to let them pass. It was audacious of them to march past Rajput territory with the captured Hindus and the treasures of Somnath. Jaitra Singh, Maharaj Kanhadadeva's best general, was given his marching orders and they fell on the shah's forces at Sakrana.'

'Was it a decisive victory for Jalore?' Padma enquired.

'It never is!' There was an ocean of rancour in Ratan's voice. 'The timing was ripe for an attack. The shah's Mongol generals – Khabru, Yalhaq and Burraq, led by Muhammad Shah – rebelled and departed with three thousand horses. By pressing this advantage, General Jaitra could have crushed them.'

'I have heard a little about the Mongols from those girls your mother sent,' Padmavati chimed in. 'They come from a land beyond the Himalayas and are descendants of Genghis Khan and Kublai Khan, aren't they? While on their raiding expeditions, I am told they were struck by the riches of this land and decided to settle down here. Some swore their allegiance to the Delhi Sultanate and were given decent posts if they agreed to convert to Islam. But there are some among the old guard who feel they are opportunistic and not real Muslims. They have faced much discrimination, so much so that they may well have been Hindus!'

'Well, the Hindus don't exactly treat all co-religionists exactly the same, do they?' Ratan replied, stroking her hair. 'Humans are the same everywhere, irrespective of the gods they worship or the race they belong to, and all are equally incapable of rising above their petty differences. Be that as it may, the Mongols were looked at askance by hereditary Muslims. Trouble had been brewing for a while but things came to a boil when the ill-gotten gains from Gujarat had to be divided. The Mongol troops were given a smaller share, though it was their men who were usually sent first into battle or where the fighting was most fierce and dangerous.

'If that were not bad enough, they were accused of failing to hand over one-fifth of their share to the throne and subjected to exceedingly rough treatment. They tried to take one of the Khans hostage but their attack failed and they had to flee.'

'If they had joined hands with General Jaitra, they could have destroyed the entire army, freed the captives and recaptured the stolen treasures of Somnath,' Padma said, wondering why men sometimes chose to distance themselves from good sense.

'That would have been the judicious approach for both of them, but Muhammad Shah's request for sanctuary was rejected by the general. He knew his king's mind on this and refused to join hands with the Muslims or risk a Hindu soldier's life for their safety. They had no choice but to make their way to Ranthambore and throw themselves upon the mercy of Hammira Chauhan who, surprisingly, was accommodating. As for General Jaitra, who failed to take advantage of the Mongol rebellion, he conducted a paltry raid which is being celebrated in Jalore as a massive victory and managed to free the idol as well as the Hindu captives.

'Alauddin's nephew and one Malik Aizuddin, who was Nusrat Khan's brother, were killed but Ulugh and Nusrat themselves escaped and managed to regroup. Most of the treasure they looted had already been dispatched to Delhi so they did suffer losses, just not debilitating ones, and they have managed to return to their overlord to make their report. Unfortunately, Maharaj Kanhadadeva's men began well but chose to leave the endeavour half-done. Alauddin's retribution will be fierce and I predict he will turn his attention towards Ranthambore. He cannot allow Hammira to get away with harbouring traitors.'

Padmavati was silent for a while. 'I've heard of the brutality of the Khalji shah's retaliatory measures against Muhammad Shah and his fellow rebels. It is almost too horrible to repeat. They say he had the wives and children of his defecting Mongol generals paraded naked around the fort, beaten, tortured and executed.'

'Even that would have been a kindness, compared to the horrors he actually subjected them to.' Ratan sighed. 'They were stripped and beaten all right, but they had to watch their infants hurled from the parapets while the troops made sport of this atrocity by attempting to skewer the babies with their spears. And then the royal ladies were handed over to the victorious divisions, who had returned from the Gujarat conquest, as spoils of war. All of this happened before the eyes of those poor girls' parents, who were nobles in the shah's court and had been forced into giving their daughters in marriage to his new Mongol generals. Incidentally, the shah had decried this practice when Jalaluddin had introduced it ... He is quite contrary!'

'When did the world become such an evil place?' Padmavati shuddered. 'And I thought he had been at his most hateful when he murdered his father-in-law! Now he has stooped to the level of murdering babies! He will come to a bad end.'

'And hopefully it will be sooner rather than later. But in the meantime, he seems unstoppable as ever. It is strange but I admire the man, his strength and willingness to do whatever it takes to see an undertaking to the finish . . .' His voice trailed off. Ratan considered himself a disciplined man but he knew he lacked Alauddin's drive and ferocity.

'Remember when our wedding was fixed in Jalore?' Ratan shook his head in the negative and Padma shoved him. 'I remember that Maharaj Kanhadadeva was talking about a possible alliance between Jalore, Ranthambore and Chittor. What happened to all of that? The shah was always the common enemy and surely by joining hands you can crush him with ease.'

Ratan shook his head wearily. 'Before Alauddin began his conquest for domination, Hammira had charted a similar course for himself. In the process, though his aggressive policy met with success, he made himself a lot of enemies among our people. He tried to reclaim much of the Sapadalaksha territory that had originally belonged to his ancestors. Even Chittor did not escape his predatory intent. Our forces threw him back but we suffered heavy casualties, and people in these parts have long memories. We haven't forgotten or forgiven Hammira, more's the pity.' *Besides, he had wanted to get his grubby paws on you and became infuriated when Maharaj Kanhadadeva decided he wasn't worthy of a goddess like you.*

But there is more, he mused to himself, *the truth is we dare not risk open war with Alauddin Khalji's superbly trained armies who function as a single cohesive unit, unlike us with our sprawling, unwieldy forces where every single soldier is keen to show off his prowess instead of bothering with teamwork.*

Padma was relieved that her father and her uncle were safe and sound in Siwana. She was sorry their conversation had taken such a sombre turn. Ratan seemed unusually pensive and her heart went out to him.

'Truth be told, at heart we are all no different from Alauddin and every bit as avaricious,' Ratan said. 'All of us have an eye on the wealth and land of our neighbours, and at the first sign of trouble in any kingdom, we behave like vultures and hyenas fighting for whatever choice morsels are available. The carrion birds are already circling around the carcass of Gujarat.'

'There is all the difference in the world between the likes of Alauddin Khalji and us,' Padma chided him. 'We don't murder babies and we treat captured soldiers with consideration. Nor do we tear down their mosques and burn their homes.'

Ratan did not want to tell her anything at first and

have her become as disillusioned as he was, but he could not resist.

'We too have raped their women, killed their children and the rest of the things you mentioned.' His tone was scornful. 'In fact, Hammira Chauhan was so furious when he heard what had been done to his new friends' families, he immediately commanded that the Muslim women who had been taken captive during the rebellion be forced to "sell buttermilk" to the male populace of Ranthambore. Although from what I hear, they are being made to do all the milking and getting milked, if you know what I mean ...'

'I certainly don't ... but I am sure it is something vile. However, I couldn't care less about Hammira Chauhan. When Rawal Ratan Singh attains victory, he will set a good example on how to be a gracious winner. But perhaps we can avoid a war and go on living in peace. Unlike Ranthambore, Chittor has not provoked the Khalji shah in any way—'

Ratan cut her off. It was time she was prepared to face the inevitable, even though he was determined to shield her from the worst of it.

'Even if that were the case, Chittor is too strategically important and wealthy to be left alone. Besides, when Maharaj Kanhadadeva refused them passage through Jalore he warned me they would attempt to cross through Mewar. Our troops were waiting to harry them mercilessly and there was many a skirmish. The shah will use that or some other trumped-up charge to declare war on us eventually. There is no avoiding it.'

'Great though the odds may be against you, Rawal Ratan Singh's triumph will be even greater,' she said confidently. 'I know that you dream of a unified land free from strife. Believe me, once you have taken Delhi after defeating and capturing Alauddin as well as his Khans, you can work towards making the seemingly impossible a perfect reality. If anybody can make this miracle happen, it is you!'

Her words were filled with so much faith, it shattered what remained of Rawal Ratan Singh's broken heart.

19

Padma's Vision

It may have started as a means of escape but Padmavati found herself feeling much better every time she visited the gods and goddesses in their temples, entreating them to watch over her husband as well as Chittor and to tide them over the impending crisis. Which was how she found herself in the Kalika temple on ammavasin for Chandi puja to invoke the blessings of the warrior goddess and beseech her to grant them victory in battle.

She was somewhat on edge. It could have been because many goats had been sacrificed and their bleating sounded exactly like the weeping and wailing of bereaved women. It took a lot of effort not to gnash her teeth. The priests were reciting thousands of verses to awaken the primordial energy of the goddess and imbue the men with her unstoppable force and ferocity.

They poured oblations into the flames and Padmavati, lulled by the heavy smoke and sonorous chanting, felt herself gradually sink into a torpor. The flames danced before her reddened eyes and she watched mesmerized as they beckoned to her, urging her to draw ever closer, inviting her to plunge into the very heart of the prancing heat.

Bathed in the rosy glow, Rani Padmavati looked more alluring than ever and Agni, the Fire God, reached for her. Panicking, she tried to flee but her flesh seemed to be melting and she stood rooted to the spot. He took her in his scorching embrace and the tongues of flames roved over every inch of her. Wracked with agonizing pain which she wouldn't have wished on even the worst of their enemies, Padma howled in mortal anguish.

Tossed this way and that in an ocean of agony, she saw them both at the very heart of her torment – the primordial mother and father – as they copulated to the cosmic rhythms that governed all in existence. Their coupling grew more and more frenzied, raw power emanating from their sweat-slicked bodies in waves. Caught up in the swirling mass of heat and energy, she was torn away from herself and everything else in her existence.

Exhilaration surged through her veins as their power washed over her and she laughed out loud. She had done it! In her hands, she held an indestructible weapon that would annihilate adversaries and everyone who wished her loved ones harm. Using the secrets she had unearthed, she would smoke out the enemies who lay in wait and snuff them out. It was the power of mrityunjaya, wielded by Shiva himself, and would conquer death. In her hands was the power to deliver her lord, husband and her people from evil.

The heat scorched her body and pain devoured her from inside, but she would not relinquish her hold. Even when she felt herself torn apart by the arrows that fell thick and fast in a relentless torrent as the battle raged fiercely all around her. Desperately, she searched for his dear face. He had to be saved and their people as well! Except the gift she bore was death and it could not discriminate.

So she swooped into their midst and killed them all. Laughter erupted out of her in gales as the weapons she wielded from a thousand arms took more lives than she could count. Sinking her fangs into exposed throats she grew drunk on fresh blood and feasted on flesh. Then she tore off her bloodied clothes and danced on the corpses that lay in all directions.

Mother and Father. Uncle Sthaladeva. Maitreyi. Ratan. They all lay at her feet. Her weapons had made short work of them all. And she danced on, inebriated, filled to the brim with death, and still she wanted more.

The battle raged on. The flames devoured everything with a ravenous appetite that could never be assuaged. Death and destruction prevailed over everything, even the impenetrable walls of the ancient citadel. Leaving nothing behind but pain and mourning. And ashes.

A girl stood tall and proud as the flames towered over her. The flames licked at her tears, drying them.

Her skin was milky white and perfect. All around, they prostrated themselves at her feet, worshipping her the way they would a goddess. Her eyes, dark and intense, were looking into the distance. Searching for her hero. She tried to call out to him but the wind snatched the words from her and swallowed them whole, leaving them unsaid. 'Father! Don't leave me! Take me with you.'

'Child of my blood! Child of my heart! Gladly would I bear you away in my arms if honour allowed it. Have faith, my dearest one. We go to the same destination. Where all souls must go when they are set free. Farewell, my love!'

His honour had not saved him. He died just the same as the ones who had lived in dishonour. Death would not discriminate. It could not. It should not.

The flames consumed her then. They inflamed every atom of her being, and anguish held her captive long after she could no longer bear it. It turned her dreams to ash. The love she had to share was reduced to cinders. Unfulfilled potential was incinerated. In the end, everything died. All that remained were the ashes. Till the wind scattered them, leaving nothing behind.

Later, they told her that her screams had resounded to the very heavens. That she had sunk to the floor in a hysterical fit and could not be revived. It was only when the Rawal took her in his arms that she quietened down. They did not have to tell her that she had sobbed quietly into his chest. That he had stayed by her side and held her close till she was calm again.

20

Wolf at the Door

Chittor was agog with the news. ALAUDDIN KHALJI WAS DEAD!

It was too good to be true and they dared not believe it till there was definitive news from Delhi. Even so, there was good cheer in the air and people breathed easier. Mothers were relieved they no longer had to tell their children that Alauddin Khalji would come and carry them away if they did not behave. Instead, they told them delightedly (and somewhat prematurely) that Yama had carried the shah away to punish him for *his* bad behaviour.

Trouble had been knocking at the shah's door for a while now. The Mongols were the first to test his mettle. Led by Qutlugh Khwaja, they had decided it was time to help themselves to more of the rich booty the land beyond the Indus offered, and had marched over a period of six months with an army that was a hundred thousand-strong to challenge Alauddin at Delhi. The shah, who could be accused of many things but certainly not cowardice, barely blinked and responded to the threat by gathering his own army to meet the Mongol hordes at Kili.

Padmavati was convinced her prayers had been answered while Ratan, as always, was more circumspect.

'I hear the Mongol hordes presented the shah with Zafar Khan's head and sacks full of the ears of the regiment they had crushed,' she said gleefully. 'Things are looking bleak for the tyrant, wouldn't you say? His empire is already crumbling and if the Mongols defeat him, it will be a death blow to his boundless ambition.'

Ratan said nothing but he did not share his wife's enthusiasm. Besides, he had developed a sneaking admiration for his enemy. The fallen Zafar Khan had been a lowly soldier, hand-picked by Alauddin because of his bravery and skill with the bow. He had risen rapidly to the rank of general. Ratan's intelligence officers had reported that a eunuch named Malik Kafur, who had been captured at Khambayat and was a converted Hindu, had seen a sea of change in his fortunes and was now the shah's personal adviser. Then there was Amir Khusrau, the poet, who had been commissioned to preserve the accounts of his many victories, one of the many talented artists the shah patronized.

'There is much we can learn from an adversary,' he said. 'We need to start looking past a man's birth or caste and find those who have the talent and capability, instead of holding them down. Thanks to the sacrifice of men like Zafar, who has repaid the trust and favour the shah has shown him, Alauddin may just triumph over the Mongols.'

And Alauddin did just that. Realizing they were up against a formidable standing army, probably the best and most disciplined in all of Asia, the Mongols had tried to draw the shah into battle at a site of their choosing, hoping to trap him, but Alauddin was too canny to be tricked. It was Qutlugh who blinked first and decided it was time to beat a strategic retreat. The Khalji men allowed them to depart as swiftly as they had come, glad that the conflict had not escalated to a full-blown war which neither wanted. It was a massive triumph for Alauddin Khalji and he was hailed as a hero by his subjects at Delhi.

Padma was disappointed but still hopeful. 'Hammira continues to defy the shah. Ranthambore will not cave in as easily as Gujarat.'

'The Chauhan king is no Rai Karan,' Ratan concurred. 'The advances of the Muhammadans have been checked twice already at Banas and in the passes of the Hindu Kush, thanks to Hammira's efforts. More of their women are "selling buttermilk" now. The victories have cost him dearly, but the good news is that the odious Nusrat Khan is dead. A freak shot from a maghrib got him in the eye. The bad news is that Alauddin has decided to lead the next attack himself.'

If Ranthambore falls, Chittor will be his next target, Ratan thought to himself. *We will defend ourselves to the best of our ability, but will it be enough?* He did not dare answer his own question.

It was at Tilpat, while on his way to Ranthambore, that the Khalji shah was supposedly slain by an assassin's arrow. Early reports indicated it was his own nephew, Akat Khan, who had killed him and claimed the Delhi throne.

Padmavati had been fervently offering her immense gratitude to the gods when the news reached them.

'Alauddin Khalji is not dead,' Ratan said without preamble, 'but his bumbling fool of a nephew certainly is. He merely wounded the shah and, without bothering to check if his uncle was dead, returned to the camp to claim the throne as well as the harem. The eunuchs barred his entry, refusing to believe that Alauddin had been killed by a drunkard like Akat. In no time, the shah was marching back to camp and his nephew fled. He was hunted down and soon the troops presented to their king his nephew's head mounted on a spear. Alauddin was amused and decreed that the grisly token be displayed all over his realm to impress upon his subjects that it does not pay to be a traitor.'

Padma was crushed. If she did not know better, she would have said the gods insisted on favouring Alauddin.

'You said he was gravely wounded,' she began. 'The shah must be in no condition to see the siege through at Ranthambore.'

'He is camped outside the fortress even as we speak. It is a matter of pride for him. The shah has already sent an offer to Hammira: four lakhs of gold moguls, four hundred elephants, the hand of his daughter Devalla Devi, and the four traitors in chains in exchange for his prompt withdrawal. Of course, he must also swear allegiance to the Delhi throne.'

'Some offer!' Padma sighed. 'Does Maharaj Hammira have any choice in the matter?'

'There is always a choice, but he is a Rajput. Hammira Chauhan will choose death.'

Padmavati remembered her vision and the girl who had called out to her father. Suddenly, she was more terrified than she had ever been in her life.

21

Ranthambore Falls

When the news reached them six months later, Padmavati wept. Hammira had ultimately been betrayed by the men who were closest to him – generals Ranmal and Ratipal among others from his inner circle. Hammira's daughter Devalla Devi had committed jauhar. Nobody was sure about Hammira's fate but the only thing everybody knew for certain was that he was dead. Some said he had fallen in battle while there were others who claimed he had been captured and chose to kill himself. Either way his remains were treated with the respect due to a fallen king.

Brave Muhammad Shah followed him not long after when he famously informed Alauddin – who had wanted to know what he would choose to do if his life were to be spared – 'I will find a way to kill you and restore Ranthambore to Maharaj Hammira's descendants.'

They said the Khalji shah had been so impressed and filled with admiration when he gave the order for Muhammad Shah to be crushed under the feet of a war elephant, there were tears in his eyes. The bards were already composing panegyrics about his tender heart.

'He is a strange man ...' Ratan marvelled. 'He insisted the remains of Hammira and Muhammad Shah be treated with respect and due funerary rites be performed. Apparently, the shah admires brave men, although it clearly does not deter him from killing them. The same consideration was not extended to Ranmal and Ratipal. He had them and their followers publicly flayed before they were put to death.'

Padmavati was listening with only half an ear. Her thoughts were with Princess Devalla Devi who had been little more than a girl when Agni had devoured her whole. Padma remembered her from the vision, or whatever it was she had seen that day in the temple. She remembered the excruciating agony of the flames, and suddenly she was angry with both Alauddin and Hammira. The former for pushing them all into such desperate straits and the latter for making the choices he had.

'Why did Hammira's lousy generals have to betray him?' Padma wailed.

'It is incredible that they held out as long as they did, but in a way it was inevitable. They were short of every necessity and the situation was truly desperate. Our informers say that Hammira had become increasingly irascible towards the end, giving orders to blind or castrate his advisers when they failed to give him answers that would save them all, accusing them of lacking political vision and criminal impotence. Needless to say, some couldn't wait to defect.'

'Would it have been so bad if Hammira had sued for peace?' There was an alien tremor in her voice. 'Was all of this necessary? I understand he was being loyal to his friends but were four lives which were forfeit anyway worth the subsequent loss of forty thousand lives? Devalla Devi was only a child . . . Surely, the sacrificial flames could not have been the only acceptable solution? If she had married the shah, Devalla would have lived out her days in relative comfort.'

'Don't judge Hammira so harshly. The man did what he thought was the best in an execrable situation.' Ratan sounded desolate. 'Most of us cannot do better than that. As for the princess, I agree what happened to her is lamentable.'

Padma knew that despite his differences with Hammira, Ratan felt strongly about his defeat and death. He had suggested they send a token force to render aid to Ranthambore against the Khalji forces, but the army chiefs had stubbornly refused. They would gladly give up their lives for Chittor and the Rawal, but not for Hammira.

She realized she had become lost in her thoughts and Ratan was waving his hand in front of her face to recapture her attention.

'I was listening to you . . .' she insisted. 'We were discussing Devalla Devi's fate. Death by fire must be the worst way to go.' She shuddered, remembering the time her sari had caught fire when she had first come to Chittor as a new bride.

'From this moment, I refuse to discuss the movements of the Khalji shah ever again. All it does is make us all feel awful and we should not waste our time, attention or thoughts on the unworthy!'

Quickly she broached a more cheerful subject that had been on her mind lately. 'Did you know that a famous traveller from a country where everybody is the colour of milk with eyes that are all the hues of the rainbow arrived on the southern coastline recently? His name is . . . Malpua Poha or something equally ridiculous. The man has travelled all over the three worlds and is documenting his observations.'

'I think you mean Marco Polo from Venice!' Ratan said, amazed as always by the ability of these sheltered women to somehow reach out to the world outside.

'Venice! Venus! Who cares?' She shrugged, remembering belatedly that her mother hated it when she did that. 'He is a great favourite of Kublai Khan of Cathay, where those charming girls with silken soft hair and buttery complexion in our harem hail from. They have such soft, tiny hands and their artwork is incredible!

'Anyway,' she continued, 'they were thrilled to hear Kublai Khan's name in these parts and told me he has some sort of pleasure dome that is one of the greatest marvels in the known world, with ice caves, magical creatures, celestial nymphs and demons who are the best lovers. Promise me, once you have discharged your duties as a king, we will buy a ship at Khambayat and sail away from here. We'll let the waves carry us to all these marvels and never come back.

'This Poha also visited some Emerald Island to the south where there is a statue of Buddha that touches the sky. I hope to see it some day with you! We can meet new people, try out different cuisines, make love under the stars and swim in the sea . . . Wouldn't that be perfectly lovely? This is the sort of sensible plan we should be focusing on instead of dwelling morbidly on portents of doom.'

'It is the best plan!' Ratan agreed.

They lapsed into a comfortable silence, though neither could sleep. Both had far too much on their minds. Padma could not help thinking that time was running out for them all and she must cherish every single precious moment with Ratan, because it may just be the last one.

22

The Rumour

Padmavati was as good as her word and refused to discuss the man Chittor was so obsessed with, even when it was impossible to ignore the towering shadow he cast over them. The shah's armies were on the march and their target was Chittor. Padma still saw no need to dwell on him.

She kept herself busier than ever. With Maitreyi in tow, she took part in the war effort by raising funds to restore abandoned buildings and other dwellings, where refugees arriving at the kingdom could reside. Maitreyi was concerned when she saw the people flooding into Chittor. Despite their efforts, they simply could not feed so many mouths if they were besieged. The Rawal did not have the heart to turn away these people. Maitreyi and many others wished he had barred the gates to them.

Padma went so far as to give whatever she could from her dwindling savings and jewellery to make sure that funds were not wanting. Food from her kitchens was sent out daily to feed the poor and she participated in temple rituals beseeching the gods to give their men strength and grant them victory in war.

Her luminous face and cheerful countenance was a great morale booster for the citizens and the troops. Their love for her was greater than ever and for many her gentle presence in their midst was the highlight of their existence.

Granaries had been filled to the brim with grain and other food that had been stockpiled for the coming siege. Barley, wheat and jowar were planted, and Ratan had repaired the stone walls that linked the natural rock formations to create rainwater cisterns that would ensure they had fresh water.

Padma took note of her husband's meticulous planning and was prouder than ever.

It was around this time that Ratan's first wife Nagmati unexpectedly paid Padma a visit. She was dressed in her somewhat severe style. On her even the brightest of bandhini ghagras took on a sombre aspect, especially since she favoured heavy ornate jewellery that complemented her overall air of doom, as if she were shouldering all the burdens of the world. Padma noticed another unique quality about her dear sister. Every time she walked into a room, Nagmati could suck out all the joy from it.

They had avoided each other assiduously ever since Padma had left the harem. Now Nagmati had entered with the same eagerness one would display on being asked to step into a steaming pile of horse dung. Not bothering to mask her disapproval, she took in her surroundings – the well-lit courtyards, silver lamps, silk tapestries, stone fountains, colourful mosaic work, fresh flowers in gigantic vases and hand-painted floral motifs that shone with flecks of precious stones – with a curled lip. What she saw seemed to confirm her view that the miniature palace was the very definition of decadence and its chief occupant was the undisputed queen of rapacious covetousness.

Nagmati declined the offer of some churma with icy courtesy and seemed determined that not even a drop of water would be consumed under her hated rival's roof. Ordinarily, Padma would have considered helping herself to the deep-fried balls of sweet goodness, but she found she had lost her appetite.

'Your mother has clearly taught you a thing or two about keeping your husband firmly under your thumb . . .' Nagmati began, scrutinizing her features. 'I always assumed he would get tired of his plaything, but you have proved me wrong.'

Padmavati waited for her to get to the point. Nagmati's

vicious tongue seldom bothered her. In fact, at some point or the other, every single person in the harem had subjected Padma to the occasional jibe, taunt, hurtful word or deed. Strangely, Padma did not mind their envious darts. It gave her relief from the constant terror that coexisted with the perfect happiness she found in Ratan's arms. A near-paralysing fear that it would not last. That so much pleasure could not possibly be had without punishment. The disquiet that arose from the knowledge that every kiss or embrace could well be the last one.

Padma's features were composed and she had the cool serenity of a marble statue. But Nagmati sensed the agitation in her heart and when she smirked, it was tinged with triumph. 'Poor thing! You really thought you could have your claws in him forever, didn't you? As someone who has been at the receiving end of your cruelty all this time and suffered in silence, it gives me great pleasure to let you know that one way or the other, it will all be over soon.'

Every word out of those cruel lips was tinged with venom and Padma felt the first flutter of panic. There was a sour taste in her mouth and she could barely breathe.

'You did not think you were going to get away with stealing the happiness of so many, did you? Serves you right!' Nagmati said, her bosom heaving.

'Now that you have got all that hate off your chest,

will you tell me the purpose of your visit? Not that I am complaining, since your presence is always an occasion for much merriment . . .' Padma said sweetly.

Nagmati's laughter was a knife to her stomach. 'Always the innocent darling . . . Do not pretend you don't know what I am here for.'

Padma's confused expression threw Nagmati off. 'You have brought ruin to Chittor and here you are sitting pretty and feeding the swans, without a care in the world. It is just as I suspected. Soon you will be Alauddin Khalji's mistress and I am sure you will be playing the same games in his palace at Siri–'

Padma rose to her feet in a single, graceful movement. 'How dare you!'

'So you didn't know . . .' Nagmati smiled. 'Allow me to enlighten you. The Khalji shah has named you as the price for the freedom of Chittor. Do you remember Raghav Chetana?'

The damned woman had her at a disadvantage. She had absolutely no idea what Nagmati was raving about. What did Raghav Chetana have to do with her? Whatever had prompted her to make such a preposterous claim? Perhaps the woman had gone mad and was a danger to herself as well as others.

'Why don't I spell it all out for you?' Nagmati purred with unsettling contentment. 'Since you have been capering around all over the place without a shred of modesty and are far too shameless, many men have looked upon and lusted after the face and body that a husband alone should feast on, which no doubt was your intention all along.'

Ordinarily, Padma would have had no difficulty in dealing with Nagmati, but right now, fear fluttered in her breast.

'Raghav Chetana, trusted courtier of the king, lost his head over many women and you were one among them. When he was apprehended for his crimes, they discovered he had a secret stash of sketches, drawings and paintings that he had commissioned an unscrupulous artist to create. There were many of you, my dear. There is no need to look so shocked. You had it coming.

'The poor Rawal lost his head completely. He ordered a thousand lashes of the whip for your secret admirer and imprisoned him, fully intending to execute him. Angered at his treatment and rightfully so, since the whole thing – tempting a decent man with cheap behaviour – was your fault. Chetana approached the shah, who is known for his lascivious ways, and convinced him that you would be a worthy addition to his harem, given your superior skills in seduction.'

'You are a filthy liar!' Padma was trembling with rage. 'How dare you? You deserve to be soundly whipped for uttering such falsehoods, but clearly, you are stark, raving mad and in need of the services of the raj vaidya.'

'We will find out who the liar and traitor is soon enough. That dirty old man is marching towards Chittor, with an army that is a hundred thousand-strong, and he will be here before the new moon. All of us have been praying that the Mongol threat, which has resurfaced near Delhi, will wipe him out for good. But the shah has decided to leave his eunuch, Malik Kafur, to deal with them, and come for you instead.'

Padma was speechless; she felt her knees would give way. Nagmati was relentless. 'Now everybody will know what I have always known – that you are a woman without honour or virtue who has brought death and destruction to our doorstep. Accursed creature that you are, redeem yourself now before it is too late. Bequeath all that beauty you are so inordinately proud of to the flames, and save your husband and your home.'

Padma was silent as Nagmati carried on. 'But, of course, you'll never choose the honourable course. You would rather allow Alauddin to take you so that you can move to Delhi and surround yourself with even more riches, while pretending to be a sweet and innocent little rose.'

With that parting shot, and pleased that she had crushed her enemy to smithereens, Nagmati took her leave. It would be worth seeing Chittor burn to the ground, if only to hear the melodious notes of thousands cursing Rani Padmavati with their last breath. Even better, the nauseating love story of Rawal Ratan Singh and his pretty little painted doll would be over soon. For good.

~

When she saw how disconsolate Padma was, Maitreyi wished she had summoned the guards as had been her original intention. At the very least, she ought to have sent word to the Rawal. But for the first time in her life, even she had been too horrified with the vile things that odious woman had been spouting.

Poor Padma lay in bed, refusing to meet anyone. She would eat nothing either. She paced her room occasionally, pausing to stare into the distance, lost in her thoughts. Maitreyi was not surprised when the Rawal materialized by her side. He always knew when his wife needed him.

'I hear Nagmati paid you a visit,' he began, 'and the two of you embraced and conversed like long-lost sisters. The entire seraglio was betting you would attempt to tear out each other's hair by the fistful.'

'You shouldn't play the clown, Your Royal Highness, when there are such serious matters afoot!' she said sternly. The sight of his dear face made her feel much better, even though the horrid feeling in the pit of her stomach refused to dissipate. 'That woman is lucky I have such a sweet and kind disposition, otherwise I would have ordered the guards to tear out her tongue and toss it into the bottom of the lake for the fish to make themselves sick with. What on earth did she mean by saying such awful things? And what is all this about Raghav Chetana and the rest of it?'

Ratan closed his eyes. *Damn Nagmati!* If Alauddin had indeed proposed such ludicrous terms, he would have been delighted to hand over his first wife and wish the shah the very best of luck as he would be needing it to deal with her.

Padma tugged on his sleeve and he sighed. 'The shah has left Malik to hold the fort at Delhi and fully intends to take Chittor. Raghav has been seen as part of the shah's entourage and will no doubt be paid in full for his treachery. The rest of Nagmati's raving was utter nonsense and I suggest you put it out of your mind. Nobody capable of rational thought would give any credence to her blabbering.'

Alas, he could not have been more wrong. The rumour grew wings and soon people were thronging the palace to declare their love and support for their queen, promising to die on her behalf. They called down the wrath of the gods on Alauddin Khalji, begging them to strike down the lustful shah. Pandemonium raged in Chittor as more and more people flocked in seeking the safety of its walls. And every single day, the shah drew closer, allegedly to carry away their beloved Rani Padmavati.

~

Reinforcements from Jalore and Siwana were the first to arrive. Maharaj Kanhadadeva and Sthaladeva sent contingents of their best troops led by two of their local heroes – Gora and Badal. They came armed with the finest weaponry, but more importantly, bullock carts loaded with fresh produce, dried and salted meat as well as fodder for the cattle and horses to help withstand the siege. Padma knew Leelavati's hand when she saw it and her eyes moistened as she wondered if she would see her mother again.

Meanwhile, the crowds sang their praises: 'Jai Rawal Ratan Singh!' and 'Long live Rani Padmavati!'

Support poured in from the other Rajput clans as well – Rathods, Hunas, Chavadas, Hariyads, Dodiyas, and the Nikhumbas – to whom the Rawal had formerly extended the hand of friendship and cemented a lasting relationship over the years by dint of favours and goodwill. The Bhils, their tribal friends from the hilly regions in the south of Mewar, Magra and Bhumat, had arrived to show their solidarity with Chittor. Things had not always been rosy between Mewar and the Bhils, but the Rawal had won them over and they had established a relationship which would have ensured prosperity and peace in the immediate future for both.

Chittor's most important ally was Rana Lakshman Singh of Sisodia who arrived with his eight sons, a tremendous gesture of goodwill, given the bloody history between the two branches of the Guhilot family. Ratan had told Padma some of it:

'Nobody is certain what exactly happened because it was so long ago. All that is known is that Rawal Karan had three sons – Mahap, Rahap and Kshem. For reasons unknown to their descendants, the two elder sons left the then capital, Ahar, and carved out their own kingdoms in Dungarpur and Sisodia, while Kshem ascended the Ahar throne. It was Kshem's descendant, Rawal Jaitra Singh, who reclaimed Chittor and restored it to us. As for the Rana, he is a direct descendant of Rahap.

'My father and Lakshmanji, to their great surprise, found that they got along well. Father told me that his happiest memories include Rana Lakshman and the days when they would go drinking and whoring together. But that was before they went on to become the most morally upstanding rulers of all time. We have been on the best of terms ever since.'

Padma wished they had met under happier circumstances and she could have gotten to know Rana Lakshman and his eight sons better. Lakshmanji was dashing, leonine and so dignified and gracious it was hard to believe he could have ever whored. He could be charming too and always referred to her as the 'jewel of Chittor', even if Nagmati was in the vicinity shooting dark looks that could curdle milk. For that alone, Padma loved him.

Despite his advanced years, the Rana was indefatigable as he and Ratan oversaw the defence of Chittor. There were trenches to be dug, booby traps to be set and the strategic deployment of their troops, who would be stationed at various points along which the enemy must advance with orders to do everything in their power to harry the opposite camp and hinder their progress. Contingents of chosen men lay in ambush, waiting to attack the supply line and burn the crops, though the Rawal forbade them from poisoning the wells and other waterbodies en route to Chittor.

'We must not poison Mother Earth; it will make monsters of us,' he insisted, and even though the Rawal's ministers grumbled, his orders were carried out.

While Ratan was busy with Lakshman, Padma had

to content herself with the news of their activities and the measures that were being implemented to save Chittor. Every time she prayed, Padma begged the gods to watch over Ratan and bless him with the triumph and glory he richly deserved. She made it a point to include Lakshmanji and his family in her prayers, and asked that they be kept safe. For selflessness such as theirs ought not to be repaid with death, however glorious on the battlefield.

And lastly, she prayed for herself. Padma asked for strength to keep her encroaching fear at bay and prove herself worthy of withstanding the crisis that was about to confront them.

23

Victory

Alauddin Khalji was resting comfortably within the confines of his luxurious tent with its grand pavilion, away from the sweltering heat. Nearly three years after his victory at Ranthambore in 1300 BCE, another sweet and successful conquest was well within his grasp. He was sipping on a drink made with sugared pomegranate pulp and rose petals, watching as Raghav Chetana whimpered within the iron cage that held him. The man was unrecognizable after the torturers had finished with him. Alauddin had ordered that he be taken along for the siege of Chittor and his men had brought in the wretch for his inspection. Together they would watch the capital of Mewar burn and then the traitor could join his damned compatriots in hell.

Rawal Ratan Singh had proved to be an extraordinarily

disappointing adversary. Initially, Alauddin had been inclined to dismiss him as a fool like the late Jalaluddin who had treated his enemies with clemency. It boggled the mind that despite knowing what he did to Senapati Dhanpal, the Rawal had let the man live and make plans to revolt against his king. And if that were not bad enough, he had not ridden out to crush them like the vermin they were.

Now he was holed up within the fortress and it was only a matter of time before Alauddin sacked Chittor and annihilated the Rawal's paltry resistance. Even Hammira had offered better sport and earned his admiration for a certain reckless courage that was foolish but extremely entertaining.

Hammira's daughter had burnt herself alive to avoid being raped and dishonoured by her father's conqueror. Her deed had made Alauddin's blood boil. He may have done the occasional reprehensibly violent deed but he had never ever touched a woman against her will. Why, he didn't even like the conniving creatures of the fairer sex, with their painted smiles that hid the sting they were about to impart, and had to fight off the many who threw themselves at him, hoping to seduce him into bestowing his favour and largesse upon them. Even Rai Karan's wife had given herself to him of her own volition.

Alauddin had ordered his scribes to decry this beastly

practice in the most strident terms. And the Rajputs called him a barbarian who was evil beyond measure, when they themselves engaged in this despicable practice which would make them accursed in the eyes of God! Now, the people of Chittor, led by their incompetent Rawal, were foolishly fighting him believing they were protecting their queen from his lust. Hopefully, this vaunted beauty would have the sense to realize that she was better off with him than her useless husband. Once the walls of the fortress came down, his men would hasten to ensure that the ladies did not unnecessarily throw their lives away and tarnish his own impeccable legacy.

Alauddin glanced up at the overcast sky. The pestilential monsoon was nearly upon them and he was determined to bring the siege of Chittor to a speedy conclusion. His men had their orders and the sooner this business was done with the quicker he could get away from these ridiculous so-called kings who allowed their women to burn.

24

Besieged

The siege of Chittor had begun. It dragged on interminably for months, sapping the people's will and draining their strength. Years of trepidation and premonitions of an approaching menace had finally caught up with them. It should have been a relief from the tortured waiting, except it wasn't; it was by far worse than anything they had ever experienced. All the preparations of the past months ought to have inured them from the horrors of a long-drawn-out siege. Except that hadn't been enough. Not nearly enough.

Alauddin's towering presence right outside the fortress demoralized the people, as they remembered the tales of his formidable victories against mighty adversaries. The atmosphere grew funereal and there were dark predictions that he would tear down their stone walls as though they were made of paper, if that was what it took for him to possess their beloved and chaste Rani Padmavati.

'Our rani will die before surrendering her virtue!' they whispered to each other.

There were wild lamentations over her fate and theirs. Padma was distraught when these rumours were reported to her and she begged the well-meaning informants to spare her the sordid details of such spurious talk that took such unforgivable liberties with her name. Not that it made any difference to the dirge people had composed in her honour, even though there was much else to mourn about. Some even commiserated with her, saying that in their opinion she wasn't entirely to blame for drawing Alauddin Khalji's evil eye towards Chittor.

Chittor was also reeling with disease and starvation. There were nearly thirty thousand people in the city. Even on bare minimal rations, the resources in the city granary had been quickly depleted. Rioting broke out over scraps of food and the soldiers had to restore order at spearpoint. The starving livestock died in droves. Some of these ended up in cooking pots but many were left to rot and the flies swarmed over their reeking, bloated bodies.

Outside the fort walls, the Muhammadans pounded their war drums, a constant reminder of their presence.

Aware that the countless privations they were enduring were far better than being invaded by bloodthirsty warriors who were baying for their blood and, given the chance, would slaughter, pillage and rape their people, the citizens of Chittor – be they slaves, beggars, whores or of royal birth – had no choice but to persevere.

They were all emaciated and worn out by constant dread. The children no longer played, laughed or clamoured for stories about the monster who wanted their Rani Padmavati.

The royal ladies were sequestered in their quarters and forbidden from venturing out under any circumstances. Sentries had been posted for their care and protection. Dhruva Rani was ailing, even though she insisted she was strong enough to teach the Muhammadans a thing or two.

Padma had requested and obtained permission to care for the old matriarch. Earlier, she would not have ever thought it possible that her mother-in-law could be such a great source of comfort. Her ancient limbs had withered away and she had to be cared for like a baby, but Padmavati did not mind. It gave her something to do and distracted her from the horrors of the siege.

Dhruva Rani would not allow sickness to mellow her and was as acerbic as ever. The only sign that she had softened was when she told Padma that she wasn't completely useless. Padma still sent out slaves with food from her kitchens, even if it was an increasingly watery gruel, to be distributed among the children who had been rounded up in the Uvar Devi temple prior to the siege. Her mother-in-law was convinced this wasting of precious supplies on the wretched was a monumental folly and lost no time in expressing her opinion. 'To the best of my knowledge, when the Creator bestows beauty he tends to scrimp on brains, but it is the purest of ill luck that he chose to deprive you of both before foisting you on my dear son.' She chortled merrily at her joke and even Padma was pleased that at least some things in life would never change.

People still gathered in front of Padma's palace, hoping for food or to seek her blessings. Mostly though they came by to express their love and swear they would die before allowing her to fall victim to the shah's lust. Their shouting made her morose and she almost always retired to her private chambers to brood.

Dhruva Rani took her despondence personally. 'Why do you get so hot and bothered every time the mob screams their rubbish?' she enquired. 'I know your mother failed to school you in flawless conduct but I thought you would have learned to emulate my own unflappable composure by now, which is the mark of a true queen. You are every bit as full of yourself as that abominable Nagmati. Do you really think the shah has honoured us with his august presence because he is enamoured of your overexaggerated beauty? What a puffed-up, preening peacock you are!'

Her outrage brought on a fit of coughing and she drank the contents of the silver tumbler that Padma held to her lips. She resumed immediately after her breathing returned to normal. 'You should have seen me in my heyday! Why, I was so surpassingly beautiful that you would have seemed about as attractive as a diseased rat in comparison. Kings were ready to go to war over me. But that is hardly the case here. As I was saying, the shah is here with his army because he lusts after Chittor's wealth. He is certainly not here on your account.'

Her words were a great solace to Padma. It helped her battle the dread that flooded her being and threatened to spill out of her eyes in a salty torrent of undiluted terror.

The days rolled into months and still the siege continued unabated.

Padma hardly got to see Ratan any more. Her nights were long and lonely, plagued with nightmares that left her shaking and in tears, without the comfort of his arms. War was a man's game and there was precious little she could do about it. In fact, it was the only religion they seemed to truly believe in. It had created a deep chasm between them, and Padma could only watch helplessly from her side and lend whatever moral support she could.

And of course, there was the endless waiting. Dawn

did not bring relief. Only fresh horror. But every single day, she gathered her dwindling strength and used it to compose herself before setting forth to meet its demands with fresh purpose and grit.

Conditions were worsening all over the city as the siege lengthened. Bodily wastes and garbage piled up faster than they could be disposed of, leaving towering peaks of refuse that attracted even more flies and all things noxious. Soon Chittor was reeking of a sewer. Once the garbage pits were filled, people began dumping their dead, as well as their wastes, into the surging waters of the Ghambhiree river.

The citizens may have even triumphed in the face of unrelenting adversity had it not been for the mortal blow that fate struck them. It was a hidden foe far deadlier than those who waited outside for them. They did not see it coming, and in their already weakened state they had absolutely nothing to fight back with. Mercilessly, they were mowed down by this new enemy that tore through the populace in unrelenting waves till the death toll ran into thousands.

The rains had started and that was when people started to fall really sick. And then cholera struck.

It started with the early symptoms of diarrhoea and dysentery. The victims would console themselves that it was merely something they had eaten. Then their besieged bodies would begin purging in earnest and soon, none would have the strength to squat, weakened as they were from defecating their strength away. The liquid faeces spurted out with explosive force wherever they lay huddled, unable to fend for themselves, and foul-smelling urine ran down their legs, burning their privates with its corrosive quality.

Then came the cramps which set fire to muscles most didn't even know they had. Tormented by unbearable thirst, the victims begged for water and dreamed of it as they sank into delirium. Fresh water was scarce and whatever little they had, they retched it right out or expelled it from the nether orifice with bright gobs of blood.

In the final stage, the shrivelled, hopelessly tormented bodies would be wracked with convulsions and limbs would be contorted to impossible angles, further compounding their misery. They would thrash violently in one final reflexive resistance against death before it quietened them for good.

Maitreyi and Padma refused to submit to this dreaded foe. The ladies of the harem and their maids wilted under the onslaught. Those who were infected were isolated in one wing of the harem to try and contain the disease. Mostly, only the very young responded to their ministrations and survived. But wives, concubines and their maids died together, united in their wretchedness and too far gone to hear Padma's gentle words of comfort and hope. Disposing of their bodies was problematic; they sewed the remains into gunny bags and laid them out in neat rows in a large room.

Just when the epidemic was dying out, Maitreyi fell ill. Padma cared for her with her own hands. Initially, the dai resisted vehemently. 'Whatever will your mother say – the queen of Chittor wiping down befouled and puckered arses! Get away from me this instant!'

Padma ignored her and soon Maitreyi was too far gone to care.

'She probably died because of the embarrassment of you having to wipe her down rather than the disease,' Dhruva Rani remarked but not unkindly. She had made available her vast stores of knowledge to Padma, suggesting remedies from their dwindling provisions.

Cholera decimated their ranks far more quickly than any enemy force. In its perversity, it spared the old and infirm or the very young, but it struck their prime fighting units and those who led them, torturing them with the indignity of its symptoms, making them suffer till their last breath.

Even the royal folk could not perform the proper rites for the deceased since there wasn't enough wood or oil. The survivors did what they could. But still, the dead piled up in ever-increasing numbers without surcease.

When the disease had run its course, Chittor was almost a ghost town. And so it was cholera that did what the mighty Khalji shah and his formidable army had not yet managed – it broke the spine of their resistance and left them too ravaged to fight for Chittor.

It was right around this time that Padma stopped praying. The cruel caprices of the gods were more than she could bear. Defeat loomed over them and she knew that not even a miracle could save them now. The knowledge brought resignation and forced acceptance of the fate that was to be theirs. Padma wished that cholera had taken her too. At least the dead had gone to a better place.

25

The Rawal's Decision

Ratan came to her in the dead of night. He had aged considerably in the last few months. There was a profusion of grey in his hair and his face and form were showing signs of the unbearable strain he had been under.

Padma had known he would come and was waiting. When he stepped into the light of the lamp, her heart skipped a beat at the sight of his rumpled hair, the texture of which she loved so much, and those shaggy brows scrunched up in worry. After all this time, simply looking at his dear face made her forget all her troubles, no matter how big they were.

Padma rushed into his arms and Ratan held her tight. He was so relieved that she had not been struck by cholera. It reinforced his decision to pursue a line of action that went against the very grain of Rajput conduct.

His wife clung to him, equally relieved that her lord was safe and alive. She wanted to disappear into his being and remain there.

Reluctantly, he disentangled himself from her embrace. He gently twirled a lock of her hair with his finger and looked deep into her eyes, almost as if he wanted to memorize every single detail of her face.

'Padma! Listen carefully to what I have to say. We've held out for as long as we could, but now it is all over.' His tone, calm as always, lessened the impact of the terrible things he was saying. 'The epidemic has almost wiped us out. My best men have shat their lives away and are long gone. We were heavily outnumbered to start with, but with this near-complete annihilation of our defences, it is not possible to withstand the siege for much longer.'

Padma nodded. She supposed she had known it all along, though none of them could have predicted such an abysmal turn of events. 'Are you considering discussing the terms of a surrender?' she asked him hesitantly. 'I remember you told me the shah and his men are usually content with gold . . .'

'True enough, but it isn't that simple. I will have to swear allegiance to him, serve as his vassal, and pay hefty tributes in addition to the reparations we will be forced to make for this war.' He sighed. 'And it is much too late for any of that. Our decision to defy the shah will not go unpunished.' He shook his head tiredly. 'He has declared jihad against us, and he and his mullahs will not be content till he has torn down every temple in the land and done whatever it takes to wipe out our faith. The shah himself sees it as a politically expedient move to placate the hardliners of his religion. If we surrender now, Hindus across the land will consider us traitors. Your uncle, Maharaj Kanhadadeva, will disown us both and spit in my face if he gets the chance.'

Ratan's smile was rueful but it broke Padma's heart.

'It need not be that bad . . .' she began. 'Temples can always be rebuilt. It will take more than a few zealots and their mad monarch to destroy our faith. Besides, there is no other way to save Chittor and her survivors.'

'There is another way . . .' he said, 'and the majority of my people, including Lakshmanji, are in favour of it.'

'You will throw open the gates and prepare yourselves for one final ride of glory, killing as many Muhammadans as possible before joining them there,' Padma said quietly. 'Chittor will be sacked anyway and the women and the children will face the wrath of the conquerors. Which means we will have no choice but to join our men by ascending the pyre.'

Ratan shook his head. Padma could sense something was weighing on him. She placed a hand on his shoulder and he shuddered.

'It will be as you say but I see no reason why we should waste so many lives in the name of honour when it is wiser to live to fight another day and reclaim what is ours. Which is why I have decided to call for a truce though everybody is against it and the shah himself may be unwilling to leave us in peace. My emissaries will confer with the shah shortly and hopefully we can iron out the details and get this nasty business over and done with. Then we can look towards rebuilding our lives and securing the future.'

Padma breathed a sigh of relief. 'You know I would have supported you either way. If you had made the decision to fight to the very end, I too would have taken poison and joined you on the other side. But this is the better choice.'

Ratan still couldn't meet her gaze. She felt the familiar dread seize her once again. There was something he wasn't telling her.

'All the arrangements have been made and my decision is final,' he said firmly. Suddenly, he was no longer her Ratan, but Rawal Ratan Singh. 'You will be leaving tonight. Maharaj Sthaladeva sent me two of his most trustworthy men from Siwana. Gora and Badal will be your guards and a slave will also accompany you to take care of your needs.'

'No!' Padma screamed. 'I will not go and you cannot make me! I'd rather let the flames of jauhar take me. I am no coward, Your Highness, and will not be treated like one. Whatever awaits us in the days to follow, I will be there by your side and we will face it together.'

'My orders will be carried out even if you have to be given a sleeping draught and bundled into a sack.' His tone was soft but it did little to take the sting out of his words. 'I would never abandon you but it is too dangerous for you here and I cannot risk your safety. On top of everything else, I cannot bear to lose you.'

'But you just told me that if we surrender—'

Ratan raised his hand to stop her. 'Senapati Devadutta has told me that my decision has not been well received by those who have sworn to serve their king. The situation is very precarious; there is much that can go wrong, and I have no wish to endanger your safety.' He thought back to the heated words that had been exchanged between him and what remained of his war council. There was mutiny in the ranks and anything could happen. But he wouldn't budge. A king's job was to serve the best interests of his people, even if they didn't know it themselves.

They stopped short of calling me a coward, Padma. Thanks to me, history will remember them as men who gave up their ancestral home and the accumulated wealth of centuries without even putting up a resistance. In your eyes I have always been a hero, but I will always be remembered as the one who disgraced his lineage.

'But there is no way out of here,' she insisted. 'The shah is unlikely to give your wife free passage out of here.'

'No, he won't!' Ratan explained patiently. 'Even though I have been assured that he doesn't approve of being likened to a demon who covets another's wife and has reiterated that he is no Rai Karan, I don't trust him.' For a moment, his features were flushed with anger.

Padma knew it galled him deeply that the vile rumours had not died a natural death. One of his ministers had remarked pointedly that he wouldn't want his women or daughters to become a Muhammadan's whore and would rather burn them alive. Ratan had come dangerously close to having the man hanged for opening his stupid mouth.

How had it all come to this? 'There are certain secret subterranean passages out of Chittor which we do not use unless the situation is dire,' he began. 'Hammir Singh, Rana Lakshman's grandson, has been allowed the use of one and he has been carrying out a few covert missions for me. Many of the young ones have already been evacuated, thanks to his efforts. He has also been entrusted with smuggling out as much treasure as possible. The boy is young but he is clever and resourceful. I see a bright future for him, which is why I ordered him to get away from here and not come back. He too wanted to stay here with his family, but he respected my decision in the end. Hopefully, some day he will become the ruler he was born to be. Gora and Badal will accompany you to the secret passage and get you out of here.'

'Why don't you tell me whatever it is that you are keeping from me? That is all I ask ... We have hardly ever been apart since the day we were married. Why would you want me to leave you when there is so much at stake?'

Ratan hesitated. They were running out of time but she wouldn't leave without an explanation, and despite what he said, he did not want her to be dragged to safety, kicking and screaming. 'My spies have unearthed a plot to kill you!'

Padma stared at him in surprise. What could possibly be gained by killing her? And why?

'There are some who are convinced that Alauddin Khalji is here to claim the "jewel of Chittor". And since I have revealed myself to have feet of clay, the decision has been made to disrupt my talk with the shah by forcing you to commit jauhar, whether you like it or not. If you resist, they will drug you and make you do it under duress.'

He ran his fingers through his hair. 'Another fanatical group swears by a ridiculous prophecy that was made after you collapsed at the Chandi puja. They have insisted that an offering of blood and flesh to Kalika Mata will prompt her to rid us of our foes and secure the succession for the Guhilots of the Suryavanshi clan. Apparently, only royal blood will do – Rani Padmavati and Lakshmanji's eight sons have been selected for this honour.'

'Nagmati is behind all this, isn't she?' Padma shook her head miserably. 'But it does not matter, I am not afraid to die. Living without you is a far more painful death. Don't ask it of me.'

'You will not talk any more of your willingness to die. It will not happen on my watch.' Ratan's voice throbbed with intensity. 'And we will not be separated either, for wherever you go my heart goes too. Believe me when I say that we will meet again. In this life or the next. But now, you must leave!'

Padma had wanted to tell him he was behaving like a fool, but she was focusing hard on not breaking down. There was so much they had to say to each other but like everyone and everything, time had turned against them as well, and a few hastily exchanged words of love and promise were all they would have. 'Once the situation is resolved to my satisfaction, I will send for you and we will be reunited!'

Padma wanted to delay the moment of their parting, but time had run out. Resolutely, she packed a few things into a small bag and hugged Ratan one last time. 'You are off to the Emerald Island, my love! Wait for me there, and when we are reunited we will go to Kublai Khan's pleasure dome and join the lovers who live there. Now go!'

Then Gora and Badal led her away from the home her husband had built for her.

26

Jauhar

It was dark outside but Padma's guardians were as sure-footed as mountain goats. When they were a good distance away from the palace, Padma came to a standstill. Gora and Badal thought the queen was scared and prostrated themselves at her feet, swearing to serve and protect her. This was the moment Padmavati had been waiting for.

'You will lead me to Gaumukh Kund in secret,' she said firmly to Gora, and then turned to Badal. 'And you will carry a message from me to Rani Nagmati.'

The two men hesitated. 'The Rawal's instructions were final. We have to lead you to Khambayat and safety.'

'I am Rani Padmavati of Chittor and I will never take the coward's way out.' Her voice quivered with anger and her eyes glowed liked hot coals. 'I will not abandon my husband and my people to their fate. And the man who even thinks of giving me a sleeping draught to smuggle me out of here will get a taste of my fury, and I will kill him even if it takes all of eternity!'

The two stalwart heroes trembled at her words. Without further argument, they hastened to do her bidding.

Padma walked silently along the narrow passage that led to Gaumukh Kund, a large natural tank that was fed by subterranean springs. Gora lit a torch before standing guard at the entrance. Padma opened her bag and made her preparations, watching the monsters that lurked in the shadows getting closer to her, hissing and snapping. But she was no longer afraid. Of them or her fate. When she was ready, Padmavati summoned her silent companion.

When Gora beheld her, he shivered as though in the presence of a ghost and could not stop the trembling in his knees.

'Will you honour your oath?' Padmavati demanded.

Gora sank to the ground and touched her feet.

'When Rani Nagmati arrives, I want you to depart with Badal at once. No matter what you hear, the two of you must not turn back. You must find Hammir Singh and help him resist the invaders. Fight in your king's name and never ever give up while there is life left in you. What is lost can be found again. Chittor has been a mother to us all and she is worth fighting for! No sacrifice is too great for her. Don't you forget!'

'I will carry your words in my heart as long as I live, my queen!' Gora touched her feet and she blessed him.

Just then they heard Rani Nagmati's steps. Gora left them alone, hesitating for the briefest of moments, before he walked away without looking back.

The Rawal's first wife had been reduced to skin and bones, but she had seldom looked more radiant or satisfied.

'I got your message,' she said eagerly, 'and I've come here to tell you that you've made the right decision. Your death will be just the thing to help our husband abandon his cowardly plans and fight to the finish like the valiant king he is supposed to be.'

'But he is valiant,' Padma replied, 'and the noblest, kindest man in the three worlds. It is unfortunate he has been betrayed by those who were closest to him and driven to desperate means. But it has not stopped him from doing the right thing for his people, even the ones who do not deserve his magnanimity.'

'What do you mean?' Nagmati was a picture of wounded innocence.

'Always the innocent darling . . . I must confess it is hard for me to understand people like you, who are consumed by hate and plot endlessly to destroy others. It was you who helped Raghav Chetana escape and sent him to our worst enemy. Your foul scheme has been successful and thousands have died because of it, and even more will be destroyed. Tell me, was it worth all the trouble? Are you happy now?'

'My happiness was never the point, but I did want you to be unhappy. It was my fondest hope that the shah would come here with fire and iron, kill the man who tossed me aside, strip you and parade you naked down the streets before turning you over to his men to be used and discarded. Nobody will find you beautiful or love you any more. At the very least, I wanted to watch you burn and the Rawal die a thousand deaths before the shah struck his unworthy head off!' The woman had a demented gleam in her eye.

'You will get your wish,' Padma assured her. 'But despite everything, I am grateful. It is a rare blessing to love and be loved in return. No matter how things end for Ratan and me, we will find our way back to each other. In the meantime, I am content to wait, holding on to my precious memories across time, space and distance, knowing that our love is eternal.'

Now it was Nagmati's turn to stare transfixed at Padmavati as she grabbed the lone torch held in place by an iron bracket. By the light of the flickering flames, Nagmati saw that her rival was drenched and dishevelled.

It took her a long moment to comprehend what she was seeing and when she did, her mouth opened reflexively in a silent scream.

Padmavati offered herself without hesitation to Agni who had long coveted her and the Lord of Fire accepted her sacrifice with frightening urgency, leaping off the torch and embracing her with a lover's frenzied ardour, enveloping her entire being within seconds.

Nagmati watched mesmerized, rooted to the spot. Not even when Agni's greed got the better of him and he rushed to devour her as well.

Her screams shattered the stillness of the night. Men and women rushed to the spot and saw their queen burning with the brilliance of a thousand fiery suns. They threw themselves onto the hard floor, banging their heads against it, screaming and ululating, till the ground ran with blood.

The women of Chittor tore out their hair as grief got the better of them. They threw caution to the winds, and one after another, they threw themselves into the flames with reckless abandon, Padmavati's name on their lips. Agni consumed them all with a glutton's insatiability.

The flames crackled as they rose higher and higher, lighting up the night sky with the brilliance of the precious sacrifice that had been made on that momentous night. The heavens were bathed in that ethereal glow.

Awakened by the cacophony of the wretched, the gods gathered to watch the passing of one who had been the brightest of souls to have adorned Mother Earth. They added their tears to those of the mourners and the skies wept.

~

Gora and Badal had heard the sounds of burning and cadences of the dying but neither had looked back.

They were waiting at the bustling port of Khambayat when a messenger brought them news.

Chittor had fallen.

Physically, they made for a contrasting pair. Gora was tall and wiry whereas Badal was shorter, giving the impression that he was stocky, when in reality he was just heavily muscled. But they seemed to mirror much of each other's thoughts and actions.

'The shah and Rawal Ratan Singh were supposed to meet midway between the fort and the encampment to discuss the terms of the surrender. Ever since the death of his brave queen, the Rawal seemed barely alive himself, but he was determined to lay down arms to spare his people. I was told that it was one last duty he wished to discharge as king, before going to the realm of the dead to be with his queen. All was proceeding smoothly and the shah was gracious, since victory was finally within his grasp. He commiserated with the Rawal about his recent bereavement, the cholera outbreak and even commended him for his bravery.' The messenger informed them.

'Who had accompanied the Rawal?' Gora asked in trepidation.

'His son Veer and Rana Lakshman's sons.' Their informant shook his head sadly. 'The young prince lost his head and tried to lunge at the shah with a dagger even as pleasantries were being exchanged. It was a clumsy, hopeless effort. The shah wasn't in any real danger but his bodyguards slew the prince immediately. The boy was hacked to pieces–' His voice broke off and he drank from a water skin before resuming. 'In the melee that followed, the delegation from Chittor was cut down and the Rawal was taken captive. Defenders led by Senapati Devadutta rode out in a doomed effort to rescue him. The Khalji forces took them apart before they fought their way past the gatehouse. The fort was stormed, and despite the best efforts of our people, there really wasn't much they could do to stop the Muhammadans.'

There was nothing more to be said. Gora and Badal paid the man for the information and watched as he disappeared into the crowds to get drunk and treat himself to a comely woman. All around them people went about their business, utterly unconcerned about the momentous events that had unfolded.

Gora and Badal had made a promise though and they were determined to keep it. It was time to find Hammir Singh and help him reclaim everything that had been taken from them. But before they embarked on their mission, it would not hurt to enjoy a good meal, sip some spiced wine and maybe even find a nice young woman to spend the night with. After all, life had to go on.

Epilogue: Man to Man

It had been a decade since Alauddin Khalji had become shah, and many years had passed after his conquest of Chittor. His empire had yet to rival Alexander's but it certainly was vast and sprawling. Multan, Mewar, Malwa, all of Rajputana, and Devagiri in the Deccan had been brought under his yoke. The regions to the south of the Vindhyas were presently in his line of sight.

Not that one could have the faintest notion of the inexorable passage of time while imprisoned. Ratan did not really care. It never ceased to surprise him that his heart, which belonged to Padma, continued to beat with tiresome regularity so long after she had passed.

The dungeons had been expressly designed so as not to allow a ray of sunlight to penetrate the all-consuming darkness. In fact, the blackness was so complete the prisoner wondered if they had followed through on their threat to blind him. A wooden bucket brimming with bodily wastes, which was seldom emptied, ensured that the air in the cramped space was fetid. The walls of the cell were wet with ooze and slime. Rats scampered across, closing in on him every time he shut his eyes.

They came for him without warning. The torches they held blinded him and he stumbled as they dragged him to the drier cells at the higher level. Perhaps they had decided to execute him after all. He couldn't deny that it may not be the worst thing to happen to him. They gave him some food and drink, water to wash with and fresh clothes. Then they left him alone. Without the rats to bother him, he was asleep within minutes.

He had no idea how much time had elapsed when they shook him awake and forced him onto his knees, pushing his head down to the floor. He felt the keen edge of the sword's blade on the nape of his neck, and Ratan Singh, formerly the Rawal of Chittor, waited for the killing blow.

'They call you a coward!' a familiar voice grated in his ear, and he looked up into Alauddin Khalji's intense gaze. He remembered how striking they had been from the ill-fated peace talks he had embarked on. 'Even your own people have disowned you in favour of your wife, who they foolishly believe did the brave thing by entering the flames. If your detractors have their way, and I am afraid they will, you will be remembered as an abject fool and the worst of kings who lost everything. It is a pity.' He smiled.

Ratan lay still. There was nothing for him to say. Plus, he had not spoken a word in so long he had almost forgotten how to do so. He cleared his throat which led to a bout of coughing.

The shah was solicitous and sent for some warm broth to revive him, insisting that he eat, though Ratan knew he would never be able to keep it down. 'I had given orders that you be treated with every courtesy once in Delhi but Malik Kafur felt that Rana Lakshman's ill-advised rebellion, which cost him his life and the lives of all his sons, ensured that you posed too great a threat and had you locked away in the deepest, darkest dungeon he could find. Ideally, he would have preferred to have you killed outright, or blinded at the very least, but even he dared not go that far against my wishes.'

Ratan was sorry to hear about Rana Lakshman's fate but was glad that he had ensured his grandson Hammir Singh's safety. Perhaps the youngster would somehow carry on the tradition of the Guhilot Ranas of Sisodia.

He thought he saw a glimmer of something indefinable in those eyes and realized that Alauddin Khalji was afraid of Malik Kafur. 'Kill him now, if it means saving a thousand innocent lives.' Ratan's voice was hoarse from disuse.

The shah's expression hardened, and then he burst out laughing. It was not a pleasant sound.

'You Rajputs are hilarious! No matter how soundly you lot are defeated, your infernal hauteur remains undiminished and you presume to know better than the victor.' He wiped tears of mirth from his eyes before continuing, 'I am sure you will be pleased to hear that Senapati Dhanpal and his rebels ran afoul of a few divisions of the Mongolian hordes and paid for their perfidy with blood.' He waited for a response, and Ratan would have liked to shrug but he could not quite manage it.

'It may interest you to know that Siwana and Jalore have fallen.' The shah continued, 'Sthaladeva put up an almighty effort to thwart our advance, but he was betrayed by Bayala, who led my men to the main water source of Siwana. On my instructions, they slaughtered cows by the dozen, filling the water with bovine blood, and left the carcasses to rot and defile it further.'

'I am sure Bayala did not live long enough to enjoy the fruits of his wicked deed and met the exact same fate as Raghav Chetana and the other traitors who helped you establish a mighty empire? It is said that you like to kill them using ingenious methods worthy of their foul deeds.'

The shah smiled. 'Of course! I am a man of principle and cannot abide a traitor. Jalore held out stubbornly for a while but Kanhadadeva was betrayed too, by a Dahiya

Rajput named Bika who sought to claim Jalore as a reward for his betrayal and pointed out a secret, forgotten passage into the fortress.'

'I suppose he went to a traitor's end too?'

'Yes, but not by my hand. His wife, Hiradevi, plunged a dagger into his chest. But by then it was too late for Kanhadadeva. He was a brave man, but in the end, a foolish one for not knowing when to bend the knee. History has no place for those—'

'Why are you here after all this time?' Ratan coughed again and this time he could taste blood in his mouth, which he swallowed reflexively only to gag on it.

The shah hesitated and Ratan could have sworn that his features were suffused with guilt. He was so surprised, he stopped coughing. 'I was told that despite the extreme nature of your incarceration and the discomfort you have been subjected to, you have never pleaded or begged for mercy.' Alauddin spoke slowly. 'That you always seem lost in your thoughts and remain strangely peaceful.'

Ratan said nothing.

'I supposed you must be thinking of that lovely wife of yours, who killed herself on my account. It is too bad I never got a chance to see her and assure her that my intentions were never anything less than honourable . . .'

Ratan wondered if this was his idea of an apology. Not that it mattered now. He coughed some more and blood frothed over his lips and a few drops splashed onto the stone floor. Alauddin drew back in disgust, rising at once to leave without a backward glance at the dying man. Shivering a little, Alauddin decided he must be getting old. This whole thing had been a ridiculous idea.

Alauddin Khalji was the greatest conqueror this land had seen and he would be remembered fondly by history. The miserable creature he had left behind would forever be considered a disgrace, even by his own people. He had taken everything from Ratan Singh – his power, prestige, life, and even his wife.

So why in the name of all things holy did he feel a twinge of envy for the broken man? Was it because he had the good fortune to have been loved by a virtuous woman in whose eyes he would always be a god? Not that it had done either of them much good.

If that were the case, then Alauddin Khalji had surely slipped into dotage and deserved to die like a dog. Like the men and women he had destroyed in his path to power and glory.

But as he left the dungeon and made his way out into the brilliant sunshine, Alauddin Khalji suspected that the only thing he had truly succeeded at was burning to ashes his own happiness in the flames of hatred that had consumed so much. And so many.

References

Chaurasia, R.S. (2002). *History of medieval India: From 1000 AD to 1707 AD*. New Delhi: Atlantic Publishers and Distributors.

Eraly, A. (2014). *The age of wrath: A history of the Delhi Sultanate*. Gurgaon, Haryana: Penguin Books India.

Harlan, L. (1992). *Religion and Rajput women: The ethic of protection in contemporary narratives*. Berkeley: University of California Press.

Jayapalan, N. (2001). *History of India from 1206 to 1773* (Vol 2). New Delhi: Atlantic Publishers and Distributors.

Karkra, B K. (2009). *Rani Padmini: The heroine of Chittor*. New Delhi: Rupa Publications.

Keay, J. (2000). *India: A history*. New Delhi: HarperCollins Publishers.

References

Majumdar, R.C. (2003). *Ancient India*. New Delhi: Motilal Banarsidass.

Mehta, J.L. (1986). *Advanced studies in the history of medieval India* (Vol 1: 1000–1526 AD). New Delhi: Sterling Publishers Pvt. Ltd.

Sharma, D. (2015). *Early Chauhan dynasties*. Jodhpur–Ahmedabad: Books Treasure.

Ulian, E. (2010). *Rajput*. Bloomington, IN: WestBow Press.

A Note on the Author

Anuja Chandramouli is the bestselling author of *Arjuna*, *Kamadeva*, *Shakti* and *Yama's Lieutenant*.

1

CRAFTED
FOR MOBILE
READING

*Thought you would never read a book
on mobile? Let us prove you wrong.*

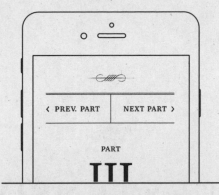

Beautiful Typography

The quality of print transferred
to your mobile. Forget ugly PDFs.

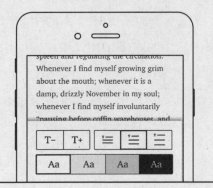

Customizable Reading

Read in the font size, spacing
and background of your liking.

AN EXTENSIVE LIBRARY

Fresh new original Juggernaut books from the likes of Sunny Leone, Twinkle Khanna, Rujuta Diwekar, William Dalrymple, Pankaj Mishra, Arundhati Roy and lots more. Plus, books from partner publishers and all the free classics you want.

DON'T JUST READ; INTERACT

We're changing the reading experience from passive to active.

3

Ask authors questions

Get all your answers from the horse's mouth.
Juggernaut authors actually reply to every
question they can.

Rate and review

Let everyone know of your favourite reads or
critique the finer points of a book – you will be
heard in a community of like-minded readers.

Gift books to friends

For a book-lover, there's no nicer gift than
a book personally picked. You can even
do it anonymously if you like.

Enjoy new book formats

Discover serials released in parts over
time, picture books including comics,
and story-bundles at discounted rates.

LOWEST PRICES & ONE-TAP BUYING

Books start at ₹10 with regular discounts and free previews.

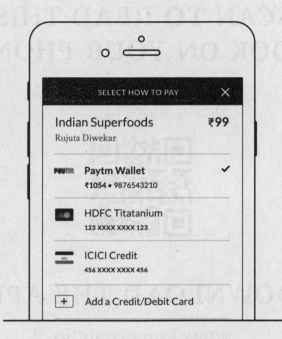

Paytm Wallet, Cards & Apple Payments

On Android, just add a Paytm Wallet once and buy any book with one tap. On iOS, pay with one tap with your iTunes-linked debit/credit card.

Click the QR Code with a QR scanner app
or type the link into the Internet browser
on your phone to download the app.

SCAN TO READ THIS BOOK ON YOUR PHONE

www.juggernaut.in

DOWNLOAD THE APP

www.juggernaut.in

For our complete catalogue, visit www.juggernaut.in
To submit your book, send a synopsis and two
sample chapters to books@juggernaut.in
For all other queries, write to contact@juggernaut.in